MURDER ON A YORKSHIRE MOOR

Breezy English mystery fiction

RIC BRADY

THE BOOK FOLKS

Published by The Book Folks

London, 2023

ISBN 978-1-80462-063-2

www.thebookfolks.com

MURDER ON A YORKSHIRE MOOR *is the first standalone mystery in this series by Ric Brady. The full list of titles, in order of publication, is as follows:*

MURDER ON A YORKSHIRE MOOR
BUTCHER ON THE MOOR
MISSING ON ILKLEY MOOR
DETECTIVE ON THE MOOR
COLD CASE ON THE MOOR

More details can be found at the back of this book.

Chapter One

Henry walked off the footpath and headed up the hill towards the drystone wall that ran along its top. Its lumps of limestone were dry and cracked in places, with some moss growing in exposed spots. These stones had sat in the field for several hundred years, come rain or shine.

The field looked out over the large village of Addingham set in the valley next to the River Wharfe. On the opposite side of the dale was Beamsley Beacon, a hill big for the area, and on its top was the old light tower, which had been used to communicate danger to the neighbouring settlements in days of old.

Henry turned his back to the view and peered up at the drystone wall. It was windy out, and the farmers were muck-spreading on the fields nearby. The sun was out but made hazy by several thin layers of cloud.

His walking boots bounced on the green grass and fresh earth as he climbed the steep incline. The muscles in his old legs were burning as he walked up the mound.

He hadn't moved this quickly in a while.

He kept his eyes on what was leaning against the wall. Was he really seeing what he thought he was seeing or was this some sort of prank? He looked about the field, just in case a film crew were nearby, but he was definitely alone.

Well, almost alone.

His dog, a small brown and white wire fox terrier, was sniffing around what they'd found. "Tessa!" he said, calling her to heel. She trotted back to him unwillingly. He didn't want her to do anything silly.

The day would be a hot one for May, but it wasn't hot yet, and it had rained heavily the previous night. The air was still cold and damp, and Henry was wearing several layers under his fleece.

He still wasn't sure he was looking at what his eyes were telling him was there, so he called out, "Hello, lad. You alright?"

The young man leaning against the wall didn't respond. His eyes were closed as if he were asleep. The side of his head rested on his shoulder, and his back was pressed against the stones.

He had dark hair, cut short, and he wore a bright blue rainproof jacket. It was the blue of his jacket that had first attracted Henry's attention. There wasn't much blue in these fields.

The young man's legs were stretched out, and he was missing a shoe. His right one. His white sock had been stained brown with mud.

Henry didn't recognise the lad from the village. He kept to himself these days and rarely bothered with the newer people who'd moved onto the housing estate. He kept in contact with his neighbours, mind. Mrs Whitehead next door knocked on every day, just after lunchtime. She needed to talk to people more than he did, and he knew she spoke to the other neighbours every day, too. She was passing on gossip about them all, but he pretended he wasn't aware of this.

Henry searched his pocket for his mobile, an old iPhone he kept in a leather case, but knew he wouldn't have any signal up here. There never was any. He'd have to walk back into the village, a three-mile walk, to get some. He looked at the young lad, lying against to the drystone wall, and said, "I'll be right back with help."

He felt terrible leaving the young man just after he'd found him. Looking around the field, he wondered how long he'd been there. People walked along the public footpaths to the south of the village near the river, but few ventured up here to the north, which led onto the hills. That was why Henry went up there.

He hadn't been up for three days as he'd been getting over a bad cough. He decided he was feeling better after having a nasty surprise on the weighing scales that morning.

He called Tessa to heel, as she was back sniffing the young man's shoe, then Henry turned around and carefully walked down the hill. He didn't want to slip and break a hip while trying to get help. Imagine the next poor sod who came through here if they found two dead bodies.

* * *

Henry left the footpath and walked through a gate with Tessa running beside his walking boots. He stepped onto the pavement that ran along the side of the road and led into the village. Trees lined one side of the road, where, beyond them, the new housing estate was. On the other side were the allotments, where he'd once had his, but gave it up as he couldn't be bothered with the upkeep. Plus, the pollen from the flowers aggravated his asthma.

A few cars passed him, going faster than the forty speed limit, as he held out his mobile in front of him. He was looking at the number of bars that showed the strength of the signal. They told him he still didn't have any.

A double-decker bus rushed past him, blowing wind and a lungful of diesel fumes into his face. He coughed and spluttered as he breathed them in. The phone signal went from 'no signal' to one bar, and he called 999.

It took a while to explain his story to the operator, as he'd been walking so fast he was out of breath. Eventually, he got the message across and said he'd be back at the spot waiting for the police, as it was hard to find. They needed an ambulance, but he didn't know how they'd get one up there. The ambulance crew would need to bring the stretcher with them, then carry the young man down. Unless they called in a helicopter, but he didn't think the local hospital had one.

He said he wasn't sure if the crime scene investigators were needed before they moved the deceased. Henry wasn't sure what the protocol was these days.

The operator said, "You don't need to stand near the deceased, sir, if you're not feeling up to it." Her voice conveyed concern for Henry, who'd coughed and wheezed throughout the call. She was probably worried about the ambulance crew having to deal with two bodies.

Henry fizzed with rage. "I can't leave that poor lad up there, can I?" He wheezed again and cursed the high pollen count and the diesel fumes. "I'm retired police, anyway, love," he said, feeling some strength coming to him. "I've seen many deceased in my time."

He rang off, telling the operator to send the police as quickly as he could. He suspected they'd send two constables from Keighley, and they shouldn't take too long to arrive. It was a dead body, after all.

He walked back to the gate and paused for a moment to get back his breath. Tessa barked next to him as if she were worried he was about to keel over. "Away with you," he said.

He searched his fleece's pockets and pulled out his blue inhaler and took two puffs. It quickly settled his chest. He was just overexcited, that was all. He'd be fine. He hoped.

Chapter Two

The young man's blue rain jacket made it easy for him to be spotted against the well-watered green grass. The lad was still slumped against the wall, like he'd been out hiking and decided to have a rest. But Henry knew better.

He walked along the footpath while Tessa ran off ahead. His calves and thighs were burning, and his chest was sore, though his coughing and wheezing had calmed down.

He blamed his near-asthma attack on the excitement of finding a body. He knew this would lead to a police investigation, and he'd not been near one of those since he retired ten years back. A few old colleagues had contacted him now and then asking for titbits, but they hadn't done so in five years. Most of his colleagues had now also retired or taken early redundancy.

He'd kept himself out of that world, telling himself he'd already given enough to it: a marriage, his relationship with his two children – whom he never saw – and his best years. Now he was happy to tinker around his house and see out the end of his twilight. He hadn't expected to make it through the pandemic, what with his bad chest, but he had. The last time he got an appointment with her, his doctor had said he was doing alright, all considering.

He walked up the hill towards the young man. He'd not moved; not that Henry expected him to, as he was pretty sure he was dead. The telltale signs were there: he wasn't breathing, and his face was a pale grey.

He wasn't a bad looker, the young man. He must have had girlfriends. Henry looked around the fields again. How did he end up here? As far as Henry knew, there wasn't anything around except for a few farms. He knew some families who owned them, but not well enough to tell if this young man belonged to them.

He unzipped his fleece to let some air in. The sun was bearing down on him now as it was nearly lunchtime, and his stomach rumbled. He'd not had much for breakfast, only two slices of brown toast with lemon curd. He could do with his tomato soup now. Plus he was missing PMQs – not that it was worth watching.

Tessa sniffed around the young man's jeans pocket, and he called her to heel, but she ignored him. "Tessa!" he said, his anger rising. She didn't move, so he stepped forward and pulled at her blue collar. "I'll put the lead on you."

She barked and let him lead her away, but then he looked at the pocket. Was there something in there? He wasn't allowed to touch the body; it could be classed as interfering with a corpse. He glanced around the fields and saw no sign of the police. Tessa barked again. There was definitely something in there.

"Bloody hell," he said, kneeling down next to the young man and pulling a pack of tissues from his fleece pocket. He took out a clean one and pulled it over his thumb and forefinger. Leaning close to the young man, he apologised, saying, "Excuse me."

He stuck his thumb and forefinger into the jeans pocket and felt a small plastic bag inside. He pulled it out and saw that the plastic bag was several inches wide and was filled with white powder. He glanced around the fields to make sure no one was coming.

No one was.

He looked back at the young man, whose head was still lolling to the side. Some strings of saliva lined his cheek. "Right," Henry said. "Is that it? Drugs?"

The young man couldn't answer.

"Then again," Henry said, "if it were drugs, the bag wouldn't be full."

The wind carried some chatter over from the next field. Eventually, two uniformed constables appeared at the foot of the hill. They'd taken off their hats and their eyes strained at the sun.

"They're here," Henry said, pushing the bag of drugs back inside the young man's pocket.

* * *

Henry didn't know the two constables. They seemed to be too young for him to. Maybe they'd joined the force within the past ten years. One was in his early forties, the other looked to be just out of training.

They both seemed unsettled by the walk from their car, which they'd parked on the main road near the gate. Their chubby faces were flush and their brows sweaty.

"You found him like this?" the older one asked. He had introduced himself as PC Brown.

"Aye," Henry said. Tessa was on her lead, and she was sitting on her haunches next to him.

PC Brown looked about the field. "Know where we are?"

"Two miles north of Addingham," Henry said. He pointed north into the hazy sky, as the sun had been covered up by fluffy white clouds. "Up there are the hills leading to Silsden." He pointed south. "Down there's the route back to Addingham."

"Yeah, but are we on some farmland?" asked PC Brown.

"I think so," said Henry. He pointed at the path leading down the hill. "There's the public footpath, but I think this is farmland."

PC Brown nodded and seemed to process the information. "Know him?" he asked.

Henry looked down at the young man. "No. Don't recognise him."

"Live in the village, do you?"

"Aye, most of my life."

PC Brown took out a spiral notebook and biro from the pocket on his black tactical vest. He flicked to a fresh page and started scribbling. "What's your name, sir?"

"Henry Ward."

PC Brown scribbled his name down with no comment. He obviously didn't know Henry. He probably was a new hire. "Alright," PC Brown said. "Can I have your contact details?"

Henry gave them to him while he watched the younger constable standing at the bottom of the hill. He was struggling to get any signal on his radio and was stomping around the field, looking out for sheep's droppings.

"You've not touched the body or searched his pockets or anything?" PC Brown asked.

Henry shook his head. "Left him as he was."

PC Brown nodded as if he believed him then put his notebook away. He kneeled down next to the young man.

"He's definitely dead if that's what you're thinking," Henry said.

PC Brown turned to look at him, his expression suggesting he felt a little patronised. "Yes," he said. "I suspected he was dead, as he hasn't moved or talked since we've been here."

"That, and he's not breathing and he's getting paler and paler."

PC Brown narrowed his eyes an instant then stood back up. His knees cracked as he hefted his weight upwards. "Right, sir. You can get off."

"Won't the detectives want to speak to me?"

"Yes, but they won't be here until the end of the day."

"End of the day?" Henry looked at the dead young man. "But you've got a body here."

PC Brown nodded. "There's no sign of foul play, so it's not a priority."

"Not a..." Henry shook his head. There was a full bag of drugs in the lad's pocket – which could have been planted – and he was left in a field where he was unlikely to be found. And this dolt couldn't see any foul play? But Henry didn't want to have to go into the fact he'd found the bag of drugs in the young man's pocket, as then he'd have to admit to looking inside it. "What about the ambulance?"

PC Brown gestured towards the younger constable. "He's on that."

Henry wasn't impressed with all this. In his day, he'd be on the scene within an hour or two once his division had got the call. A body was a body, no matter how it looked to have died. And from experience, uniformed officers weren't the best at determining this. It should be left to a trained detective. "What about his shoe?" Henry asked.

PC Brown looked down at the young man's feet. His right sock was covered with dried mud, which was starting to flake off. "Ah, yeah. I hadn't spotted that. Have you seen it anywhere?"

"No, but I can go look for it?"

PC Brown shook his head. He probably thought Henry was an old codger looking for something to do, which was only half-true. "No, that's okay, sir. You get back home and put your feet up."

"Right, well." He didn't want to go, he felt some ownership over the body. He'd found this lad in this field by chance and wanted to see him off in an ambulance. If the boy was local, he'd attend the funeral. He'd introduce himself to the boy's parents and tell them it was him who found their boy alone and dead in a field and waited with him until help came.

"Thank you for your time, Mr Ward," said PC Brown, turning his back on him.

"It's former Detective Chief Inspector Ward," Henry blurted.

He regretted it immediately as PC Brown turned back around and asked, "What did you say?"

Chapter Three

Henry had to explain that he'd been a detective chief inspector at Bradford for ten years before he retired. He didn't go into why he retired. He figured the two constables would learn about that when they got back to their station.

PC Brown nodded his head through it all, his eyes growing wider with each revelation, his cheeks getting redder. Henry had started his detective career working on the Ripper case and moved on to handle other big cases in the area, until the Bradford murders in 2010 by the self-styled 'Crossbow Killer', his last big case before he retired.

PC Brown's attitude became more emollient. He smiled a bit more. Only because he was guessing Henry knew the higher-ups in the West Yorkshire Police and was well-positioned to cause a fuss. "Right, sir," said PC Brown, his 'sir' now sounding like he was speaking to a senior officer rather than an annoying old codger. "I'll go speak to my colleague and see what we can do about getting some detectives and an ambulance here sooner."

"Don't pull them away from something important on my account," Henry said. The last thing he'd want was for some overstretched detectives to get pulled off a big case just to appease a retired SIO who'd become a busybody.

PC Brown waved him off as if to say 'for him, nothing was a problem'. He walked down the hill towards his colleague and whispered in his ear. The two constables looked up at Henry occasionally, then the younger one got out his mobile phone, probably to google Henry. Not that he'd get any signal up here.

Henry shook his head at them and turned to the dead young man. "We'll get you out of here and find out what happened to you, lad. Don't you worry." He glanced back at the two constables. "It might take a while, mind."

Eventually, PC Brown came back up the hill. The younger constable was rushing along the footpath towards their patrol car. "I've sent my colleague to radio in from the car." He was breathing heavily after walking up and down the slope. Henry wondered if PC Brown's asthma was worse than his own. "In the meantime, if you'd like to help us find that missing shoe, we'd be most grateful, sir."

Henry sighed. From rude to smarmy in a flash, this constable was suited for climbing his way up the greasy pole. He was hungry now, as well. It was well past lunchtime, and his hands were shaking a little from lack of sugar. But if he could help, he would. Besides, missing lunch wouldn't do his waistline any harm. "Fine, I'll go have a look around the neighbouring fields for that shoe."

He pulled Tessa's lead away from the body then paused. She wasn't a sniffer dog, but she was still a dog. He led her to the dead young man's muddy sock and let her sniff them.

"What you doing, sir?"

"Letting her get the scent."

Tessa barked, and he pulled her down the hill. The earth and grass were bouncy underfoot as he walked down. When he was far enough away from the dead young man, he let Tessa off her lead and continued onto the next field.

Tessa ran off ahead of him, jumping through a small opening in the drystone wall where a gate had been, and sprinted into the neighbouring field. She'd not enjoyed being on her lead while out on a walk and now she was making the most of it.

Henry looked about the area. The young man had stopped at the wall here, but where had he been going, and where had he come from? Was he walking away from the village or towards it?

Henry hadn't spotted a shoe on his way up from the village, not that he'd been looking for one. But he thought he'd have noticed a random shoe lying near the footpath. Plus, Tessa would've been all over it if they'd come across it.

The young man must've been walking down from the top of the hill, walking towards the village when he stopped by the wall. That's if he came to be there of his own volition.

Henry looked at the opening in the wall where a gate would've been. It wasn't wide enough for a car, he thought, but could a quad bike or something get through there?

He heard Tessa bark in the neighbouring field and hurried to go find her.

Had she found something?

* * *

Tessa stood barking at a dead sheep. The sheep lay on her side in the grass, her long curls of wool quivering in the breeze. She looked to have died recently, but there weren't any discernible marks on her. No blood or gore. Just a dead sheep lying alone in a field.

Henry called Tessa to heel, as she was still barking excitedly. This was turning out to be a memorable day for her, she'd found two dead bodies on her walk.

Henry struggled to kneel but managed it. The ground underneath his cord trousers was moist and cold. There was a dribble of blood around the sheep's mouth. Then he looked down and saw a large wound on her underbelly, which was the size of a fist. Flies flew around its dead black eyes, and he waved them away.

He got back up to his feet and looked around the field. There was a single-lane road to his right on the other side of the wall that went up the hill. A red Ford Ka drove down it and disappeared behind a drystone wall and some windswept trees.

There was a small hamlet of farmhouses up the hill, some of which were owned by farmers, with the others being owned by wealthier people. People who could afford to buy an old stone farmhouse and some land.

He strained his eyes in the sun, which had come back again, and looked up at the field. There were a few clumps of grass, which were being blown by the breeze, but nothing else. The wind was stronger here and carried on it the stench from the muck-spreading a few fields away. He couldn't see a stray shoe anywhere. He could continue looking for it, but he felt he wouldn't find it.

Something was going on here. Either the poor lad had fallen ill after a party on the hill and had got lost on his way home, or someone had dumped him here somehow.

He looked back at the dead sheep. "How do you fit into all this?" he asked, his voice getting blown away by the breeze. "Maybe you don't fit in at all."

He heard some chatter in the previous field and headed back to it. He called Tessa, who'd wandered off, and she ran back towards him.

The ambulance crew had arrived. The two crew members each carried one end of a red folding stretcher and placed it next to the young man, whose bright blue jacket made him stick out like a sore thumb.

One of the ambulance crew looked for vital signs, checking the young man's neck for a pulse through latex gloves, but she gave up after a few moments.

They all stepped away from the young man, and PC Brown instructed his colleague to take photos of the body on his phone, which he did. Then, one of the ambulance crew members pulled the young man's legs forwards while the other cradled his head. They eventually got him lying flat on the grass.

Tessa started barking and Henry told her to shut it. This wasn't the time to make a noise. But Tessa still made a racket. "Tessa, what the bloody hell's wrong with you?"

The ambulance crew member holding the young man shouted out, "Hang on!"

They stopped moving the young man, and PC Brown peered down at the drystone wall.

"What is it?" Henry asked, walking up the hill towards them, his calves and thighs burning. He saw it immediately and took a breath.

There was a pool of blood on the wall, which had streaked down the stones. It must've been coming from the young man's back.

"Turn him over," Henry instructed.

PC Brown stiffened, lifted his shoulders up like he was trying to make himself taller, then relayed the order to the ambulance crew.

They carefully turned the young man over. His bright blue coat had a huge red gash in it between his shoulder blades. Blood had seeped down his back.

"Bloody hell," said PC Brown.

Henry wanted to ask him if it still looked like there'd been no foul play, but he held his tongue.

This would become a bigger case than Henry had thought. Perhaps, it was the chance for him to redeem himself for his own past mistakes. A chance he believed would never materialise.

Chapter Four

Henry opened his garden gate and ordered Tessa through. His front yard looked out onto Main Street in Addingham. His small, stone Edwardian cottage was in the middle of a small terrace that curved around a corner in Main Street.

He'd lived here since he retired ten years ago, after he left his flat in the centre of Bradford; an old mill conversion that was always cold and damp. His little cottage only had one and a half bedrooms, but it was well situated. The local shop was a quick stroll on his right, and the local pub on his left, where he'd go for early doors two or three times a week. But he tried to keep a limit on his drinking these days. He didn't want to find himself in a sticky situation again.

He slammed his gate shut just as a double-decker bus rolled past and shot out a lungful of fumes from its exhaust. He coughed again, and gestured for Tessa to get to the front door while he searched his fleece pockets for his blue inhaler. He took two puffs while leaning on an old, hip-high chimney pot he'd converted into a plant container. The lavender he'd planted last year was growing out. Its violet buds filled the air with their scent.

The door to the neighbouring house opened, and Mrs Whitehead stepped outside wearing a colourful top. She had long blonde hair, which bushed out to the sides, and had wrinkles under her eyes. Apart from those markers, you wouldn't think she was in her mid-sixties she was so full of energy. She put Henry to shame with her antics, running almost every committee and charity in the village, along with being a parish councillor.

"Where've you been?" she asked, sounding slightly worried.

"I went for a walk up out of the village."

"I know," she said. "You told me that last night, and I saw you walk off first thing this morning." She shook her head like she was frustrated. "*Pointless* is nearly on now. Where've you been all day? I was getting worried sick. I was about to call your old lot to go up there looking for you." She called the police 'your old lot', marking him and them with the same mild contempt.

"I got held up," he said, leaning on the old chimney pot. He was starving, and he felt his legs and hands shake. If he didn't get anything to eat soon, he'd lose his rag and snap at her, or pass out. He preferred the latter to happen as it'd cause him less problems in the long run.

"Held up where? On a footpath?"

His hand shook the chimney pot, nearly knocking it over, and she rushed to the drystone wall that separated their two front yards. "Are you alright?"

"Yeah, fine," he said, feeling his knees give in. He let out a hollow laugh to make light of the situation. "Just hungry. I skipped lunch and have been walking a lot."

"Here," she said, matronly. "You're coming in for a sit down and a cup of tea."

"No, it's no bother."

"Henry," she said in a way that reminded him of his mother. "Get inside. I've got some fresh scones or a slice of apple pie, you can take your pick or have both. Come on."

* * *

17

He'd relented and agreed, after letting Tessa into his house – she wasn't allowed in Mrs Whitehead's because of the cat.

Mrs Whitehead had him sit on her sofa in front of the TV, which was playing BBC News on mute. Her house was almost identical to his in layout, but lighter in colour and more feminine. There were figurines on the windowsill, fluffy cushions and rugs, and the air was thick with potpourri.

She came in and handed him a cup of milky tea and a plate holding two buttered-and-jammed scones and a large slice of apple pie. "Right, thanks," he said.

She sat in a comfy chair opposite, which had a small hamper next to it full of knitting equipment. She sipped her tea and waited until he'd eaten before she started her questions.

"So, what's happened? You've been up on the moors all day, and I've seen several police cars and an ambulance drive past with their lights flashing."

He sipped his tea as the scones were quite dry. "I found a body."

Her eyebrows nearly met her hairline. "A body? Where?"

"Up out of the village, to the north, on the hill."

"Whose?"

"I don't know. Some young lad." He shrugged. "Could've been sixteen to twenty." He shook his head. Anyone under thirty looked young to him so he wasn't very good at guessing ages on sight.

"Bloody hell." She rested her finger on her dimpled chin and looked out the netted window for a moment. "How'd he die?"

He swallowed a mouthful of scone and sipped his tea before answering. "Looked to be exposure or something, until we moved him and saw a huge wound on his back."

She gasped. "He'd been killed!" She looked out the netted window again as if the killer was out there on the loose, which Henry surmised as truthful. But he doubted the killer would bother with Mrs Whitehead. "Who did it?" she asked.

"Don't know. CID are on the case, they'll find out."

"So you spoke to your old lot, then?"

He nodded. "I called them in and walked that footpath more times than my hip needed."

She shook her head. "You are retired from all this. Anyway, why didn't you ring me?"

"What could you have done?"

She shrugged. "I don't know. Something."

He lifted up his half-eaten plate. "You gave me scones, which was something."

"Aye, but I could've done more." She shook her head at her own perceived lack of input and sipped her tea. "Want any more scones?"

He put his hand over the plate. "No, thanks. It's very nice though."

She nodded. "Made them today while I was fretting about you." She shook her head. "So no idea who the young lad is?"

"I don't, as I said. Could be local." He shrugged.

"I wonder if he is. You didn't find a name on him or anything?"

He shook his head. He'd left the scene shortly after CID had arrived. A detective in her forties with a southern accent had questioned him. DI Barnes was her name. She was very curt but efficient and didn't seem to know or care who he was. She asked him a few questions, saw he was looking tired and rung out, and offered him a ride home. He declined as he didn't want Mrs Whitehead to ask him loads of questions after she saw him getting out of a patrol car. But he might as well have agreed to it now.

"I wonder who he was?" Mrs Whitehead asked again, peering out the window. "It could be the Ashfields' lad. He's young. What colour hair did the young lad you found have?"

"Dark brown."

She shook her head. "They're all blonde." She sighed. "I wonder who he is."

Henry didn't know, but he had a feeling he'd find out soon. If the young man was local, then it was only a matter of time until his family were notified, and the whole trauma would rock the village for weeks.

Chapter Five

Henry wasn't that hungry after all the scones and the hefty slice of apple pie Mrs Whitehead had fed him. But he had some kippers in the fridge that were about to go off, so he decided to have them with some toast. He had skipped lunch after all.

The TV played the local news in his living room while he was in his kitchen, heating the butter in his pan. He could almost hear the news presenter through the doorless entrance.

He had the news on in case there was any more information about the body, not that he expected a name or anything. They wouldn't give that to the press for the next day or so, until the next of kin was informed and the body identified.

After cooking the two kippers, he crumbled off the tail end of one, pulled out the thin bones, and put it in Tessa's bowl, who greedily tucked in.

He sat down on his dark green, velvet chair with a high back opposite the TV, his dinner on a tray. He'd tried to have dinner at the small, round kitchen table when he first moved in, but the table was now covered in unopened letters and old newspapers. Plus, he would just sit in this chair afterwards anyway, so why bother eating someplace else?

His thighs and calves were still aching, and his left hip was burning. He'd have to fish out those painkillers his doctor had given him or he'd be up all night in pain.

The local news mentioned that a body had been found halfway through the programme. It was a small snippet and mentioned only a few facts. A dog walker, Henry, had found a body on the hill above Addingham, and the police were investigating. That was it. They moved on to other news.

It wasn't really worth the wait, was it? He hadn't expected them to say much, but he'd expected them to say more than that.

He'd finished his meal, and was sipping at a glass of water, when there was a knock at his door. Tessa started yapping, as she did whenever someone knocked on the door.

He stood up, placing his tray on a pine dresser opposite his chair and said, "Coming." Then to Tessa he said, "Oi, stop it!"

She calmed down and he headed to the front door. He expected it to be Mrs Whitehead. She would've watched the local news and probably wanted to witter on about it. She was desperate to know who the lad was, and Henry didn't know why. He was more interested in knowing what had happened to him than who he was.

He opened the door and didn't recognise the woman standing on his doorstep.

* * *

She had dark hair, could've been a model in her youth, and looked upset. Tears were streaming down her cheeks. She sniffed as she looked Henry up and down. He guessed she was in her late forties and was about to ask who she was when she spoke first. "Are you Henry Ward?"

He nodded. "I am. Are you…?" He didn't continue his question as he didn't need an answer.

"I'm William's mum." She sniffed. Saying his name seemed difficult for her.

There was the sound of a car horn on Main Street, just beyond his drystone wall. A blue Audi was parked badly on the pavement outside Henry's gate, blocking one of the two lanes in the street.

A white van beeped its horn again, and its driver gave the woman on Henry's doorstep the finger. Henry shook his head. If only that driver knew.

"Do you want to come in?" he asked.

She shook her head. "I just wanted to know…"

Henry nodded. "Anything."

"When you found him… this morning… did he look scared?"

"Did he…?" Henry thought about it. The young lad had seemed asleep at first, not dead. It was only when Henry had walked up to him that he realised he wasn't alive. "No. He looked at peace."

She sobbed, covering her face with her hand. Henry patted his jeans pockets for a handkerchief or tissue but didn't have one. "Are you sure you don't want to come in?"

She shook her head again. "I've just been to see him."

"Right." He took a breath. From experience, he knew this was the worst time to be around the next of kin. They acted unpredictably, which was fairly understandable considering what they'd just seen. One minute they were having a dull Wednesday, the next, they're identifying the corpse of someone they'd brought into the world.

Another horn went off in the street. The badly parked Audi was causing a traffic jam. Henry noticed the car was empty, suggesting William's mum had identified her son's body on her own.

He was about to mention this when she said, "He looked scared to me, but I wasn't sure if I was seeing him right. I was in a bit of a mess." She sniffed again, sounding guilty.

There was another horn.

"I just wanted to check with you that he wasn't scared. That he was alright. The last thing I'd want for him was to be scared while he was alone in that field."

"Listen, he wasn't alone for long. I was with him the whole day, and I got him what help I could."

She looked at him through bloodshot eyes and nodded. She gripped his hand; her fingers were damp from her tears. "Thank you."

Chapter Six

Henry felt uncomfortable after William's mum had left. So that was the young man's name – William. He guessed his mum and him were local. Maybe they lived on the housing estate. She had a nice car so she could probably afford a detached three-bed up there. He wondered who she lived with. Did she and William live together? If that was the case, she was going to have a rough time of it.

He cleared up his dinner and took one of the painkillers for his hip. He sat back in his velvet chair with a strong cup of tea in hand.

His eyes kept dashing off across his small living room to the pine dresser where he kept a bottle of Scotch in the bottom cupboard. He'd kept it for emergencies and Christmas, and this felt like an emergency. But he wasn't sure having a tipple would help him. Besides, he'd just taken a pill for his hip and didn't think the two should mix.

Tessa was sat in her basket near the staircase. She was fast asleep and occasionally kicked her legs. Probably dreaming of finding more bodies, or that shoe he'd had her look for.

He sipped his tea and stared at the TV. It was some holiday programme, and he'd put it on mute as he couldn't deal with the racket. He just wanted to see faces while he sat there alone.

He didn't mind living on his own, but at times he wished he didn't.

There was another knock on his door. He checked his silver watch. It was nearly 8 p.m. Maybe it was Mrs Whitehead, though he'd expected her to knock earlier.

He placed his tea on a coaster on the side table and headed to the door. Tessa didn't even stir as he opened it, she was so comatose.

It was the blonde detective who'd questioned him earlier, but she introduced herself again as if they hadn't met.

"DI Barnes." She showed him an ID card, and he noticed they'd changed since his day. "Can I come in?"

He let her in and offered her tea, which she declined. He gestured to the two-seat sofa that ran along the far wall and wiped off some of the dog hair for her.

She was quite tall and elegant. She had short blonde hair, almost in a man's hairstyle, and long legs. She was tanned, and it seemed to be real. She wore a professional business suit that looked expensive and a crisp, clean white blouse. In her hand was a leather A4 folder, which she opened. Inside Henry saw an iPad and a notepad and pen.

She brought the iPad to life and looked through some notes while he sat himself down in his velvet chair and picked up his cup of tea.

The thought came to him that his house would reek of kippers, and he hoped she'd know it was kippers and nothing else.

Eventually she looked up from her notes, her dark blue eyes narrowing, and said, "You never said you were a DCI."

"I told the uniform officers and thought they'd tell you. Though, I suppose they kept it to themselves?"

She didn't answer. "I wasn't aware of who you were. I'm not from around here."

"Aye, I'd gathered that from your accent. From down south?"

She nodded. "I was in the Met."

"Ah." He nodded to show he was impressed, although he wasn't. The Met detectives had egos bigger than their budgets. "How'd you find yourself up here?"

"I relocated," she said with some finality. She wasn't going to say any more than that.

Was she with a Yorkshire man? He glanced at her hands and didn't see any jewellery, but that didn't mean that much these days.

"Well, I hope you like it up here."

She looked down at her notes on her iPad. "You found the body this morning?"

"William." He sipped his tea.

She looked up at him. "You know his name?"

"I had his mum at my door an hour ago."

DI Barnes seemed interested in this. "What did she say?"

"Just wanted to know how I found her son."

"What did you tell her?"

"What I thought was appropriate to tell her. That he was at peace, and I did my best for him."

She nodded as if she would've said the same then looked back at her notes. "You didn't touch the body or anything?"

"No, as I told the uniformed officers, I didn't touch him." He sipped his tea. "I do have forty years experience of crime scenes."

"I know you do. Although you've not been near one for a good ten years."

"That's true. I wasn't expecting to walk on to another one."

She turned off the iPad and rested her elbows on it. "What I don't understand, Mr Ward, is why you found the body."

"What do you mean? I was walking my dog and came across him."

"Yes, but is there more to it than that?"

He scoffed. "You must be very desperate if you're wanting to drag me into all this."

"Well, I did look at your record and read about what happened towards the end of your career."

He felt a shiver down his spine and his cheeks reddened. "That was ten years ago. I was cleared, and I left the police."

"Yes, but you weren't completely cleared. You were retired off before the inquiry could conclude. You got your full pension and kept all your commendations and some of your reputation. But most of us know what really happened, don't we?"

He sipped his tea but felt his hand shake. She noticed it.

"I think, unless you don't have any other questions pertaining to the body I found this morning, you should leave," he said.

She closed her leather folder and stood up. "We'll be in touch if we need more information, Mr Ward."

"If that's the case, do you not have a partner you can send around?"

She stopped and looked at him. There was some malice in those blue eyes of hers. "It'll be me or my partner, Mr Ward, depending on our duties." She looked about his small living room, which to him now seemed messy and uncared for. "With any hope, Mr Ward, your involvement in this case will end here, and you can spend the rest of your time in peaceful retirement."

She saw herself out and slammed the door, which woke up Tessa.

She started yapping, and Henry said, "Bit late for that now."

Chapter Seven

Henry sulked while watching Newsnight on mute. Some Labour politician was being questioned about something or other. It wasn't one he recognised. All the ones he recognised were either too old to be important or retired or dead.

He'd given in to having a tipple. DI Barnes had not only touched a nerve, she'd hit it with a mallet. He sipped the Scotch, which he was holding in a simple tumbler from IKEA. It tasted peaty and burned his mouth. It used to burn less a few years ago.

He was going to allow himself one then give up on it.

He'd not been made to think about what had happened before he retired for a while. That was one of the reasons why he avoided the police. If he could have relived today, he'd have avoided calling them. But he hadn't had the choice, had he? He couldn't have left poor William alone for someone else to find. That made him wonder if someone else had found him before Henry.

He parked that idea and sipped his tumbler again. Tessa was curled up on the leather sofa where DI Barnes had sat. She was asleep again, dead to the world.

He avoided thinking about what happened before his retirement, because it was traumatic, and it was politically motivated, he felt. Officers within his command had cut corners, they'd beaten up suspects, they'd dealt in criminality themselves – a lot of it – but they were connected with people higher up than Henry.

Regardless, it got out. Journalists sniffed around, and there were inquiries and investigations, and half of the truth was put out in the public. Some of the officers who committed real crimes were let off with sackings. The real culprits who were connected with higher-ups were left in post but told to keep their heads down.

Henry, who had served his forty years, was pensioned off quietly and the investigation into him was called off. He didn't think they'd have found anything, though. Throughout his career, he'd done his best. He wasn't a saint. He'd cut corners too, gone against procedure, roughed up suspects in the days when he could get away with it, but only if he knew the suspect was guilty and needed a little encouragement. All of it was in aid of helping right those wrongs. The wrongs that William's mum was experiencing right now. Her son, a young lad from a good home, had had his whole life in front of him. Now he lay in a morgue at BRI.

His mum was probably expecting her son to be around for the rest of her life, to help her out when she was in her twilight years and to provide her with grandchildren. She'd get none of that now. She'd get loneliness, despair, and awful anniversaries every year when this same day rolled round.

Someone had taken William's life and his mother's happy future.

Henry sipped more Scotch.

He'd have to leave well out of it. Despite being confident any inquiry into him would have cleared him, he was still worried. There was some truth in some of those accusations against him.

He knew what some of his officers were doing and received the odd bung every now and then, which he stashed away in various locations. He wasn't proud of it, and if people found out he could face prison.

He didn't fancy going in one of them at his age. He'd have to spend the rest of his days in his self-imposed prison here, his two-bed cottage. Which was nice enough, all considering.

He drained his glass and put it on the coaster on his side table. "You're not having another one," he said to himself.

He felt alive for the first time in a while. He felt several years younger, despite his hip and lungs giving him gyp. He wasn't even seventy yet, but some days felt like he was in his eighties. That was what sitting around letting your mind turn to mush did to you.

Maybe he could keep track of this investigation. Nothing that would get him in trouble or arouse DI Baine's fury, but something that ran along the side.

There wasn't anything illegal about that, was there?

* * *

He knocked on Mrs Whitehead's door just after eight in the morning. He had his fleece on as it was cold out, but there was already a bit of sun. The morning rush hour ran along Main Street as did a bus. He knocked again, expecting her to have opened her door already. Maybe she was in the shower?

He looked about her front yard which was filled with plant pots that had an assortment of flowers of all kinds of colours. There didn't seem to be any arrangement. If it was colourful and pretty, she'd have it.

Her black cat slunk in through the gaps in the gate and meowed. It sauntered up to his leg and sat there, looking at the door. Henry disliked that cat with a passion. It was a miserable, nasty little sod.

The door opened and Mrs Whitehead appeared, wearing a pink fleece; her blonde hair was wet and scraggly. She saw the cat and said, "Come in, you." She then looked at Henry. "What are you doing here?"

"Can I come in?"

She nodded. "But I'm about to dry my hair."

He sat on the sofa and heard her blow-dry her hair upstairs. *BBC Breakfast* played quietly on the TV. Her cat, Barney, had curled up next to him, leaving a foot between them. Henry knew better than stroking him. He had a scar on his left hand from when he'd first tried.

Mrs Whitehead came downstairs with her hair dry and coiffured. "What is it? Is it about that body?"

Henry nodded and pulled out a notebook he'd found in one of the drawers in his spare room. "He's called William. No last name, though."

"William?" She sat down in her comfy chair opposite the TV and placed her index finger on her dimpled chin. "Dark hair, you said?"

He nodded.

She shook her head. "Don't know a William. I know a Ryan who lives behind the pub. Glad it's not him. I know his parents."

"His mum drives a blue Audi."

She frowned then shook her head. "I know next to nothing about cars, so can't help you there." She tilted her head to the side and looked at him. "How do you know what his mum drives?"

"I saw her last night."

She slapped her hands on her thighs. "When?"

"She came over, just after the news."

She waved her hand in the air. "Don't get me started about the local news, they said sweet sod all about it. If it'd happened over there, it would've been the main headline."

Henry nodded his understanding. She meant Ilkley, the neighbouring town that had a high opinion of itself. Addingham, their village, was its poorer cousin.

"Perhaps," he said, wanting to move on as she could complain about Ilkley for hours. "I half expected you to come round after the news."

She shook her head. "You looked knackered, so I left you to get a good's night sleep. So what did she say, his mum?"

"She'd just been to identify him."

She shook her head. "Awful. Was she a mess?"

He nodded. "I wondered if she lived up on the estate."

She shrugged. "Don't know. Maybe. Like I said, I don't know a William."

"I also wanted to know if you fancied a walk."

"A walk? I'm not Tessa!"

"I know, but I don't think she can help me at the moment."

She raised one of her white eyebrows. "What's going on, Henry?"

"Nothing. I just thought it might be worth keeping an eye on things. Besides, you're a local parish councillor. It's not unheard of for you to make sure people are alright."

She pulled a face, clearly unconvinced. "What are you on about? This has nothing to do with the parish council."

"A murder in your village has nothing to do with you?"

She mumbled which sounded like she admitted it might be her problem.

"Well, I found the lad and want to make sure they get to the bottom of what happened to him."

"What is this? You don't trust your old lot to do that?"

"No," he said, "I trust them. I just want to make sure they don't miss anything."

Chapter Eight

The housing estate was at the top of the village, heading north, not too far from where Henry found William. It had been built by a property developer in the early nineties and was made up of detached two- and three-beds. They'd been expensive back when they were built and they were expensive now. The estate was surrounded by rolling hills and farmland, and it was served by one road which attached itself to Main Street near the bypass.

Henry and Mrs Whitehead walked along the pavement. She pointed out houses to him, telling Henry if the occupants had asked for planning permission. She also divulged if they were going to get it or not.

As they walked, it became apparent she didn't know many people from the estate. Despite it being a part of the village, it was pretty much on its own. People who lived there could drive in and out of the village via the northern route and didn't need to drive through the village at all.

It was around ten o'clock when Henry saw the blue Audi. It was parked on the paved driveway of a three-bed detached house. The house had a fresh green lawn and a high, varnished fence.

Henry walked up to the driveway. The curtains were drawn, and the house looked unoccupied. "Shall we knock?" he asked.

"No," Mrs Whitehead said, looking around at the neighbouring houses as if people might be watching them.

"Don't be silly," he said, walking down the driveway. "You can wish her all the best from the parish council."

She snapped at him. "Henry!"

He climbed up the three steps to the front door and rang the doorbell. He heard it echo inside the house.

"Henry!" Mrs Whitehead said again.

He turned to her and said, "She's probably asleep or has gone out."

He didn't believe she'd be out as her car was sat in the drive. Unless the police had picked her up, but he didn't think they'd be doing that yet. They'd still be getting a team together, and they'd want to leave her be for a while.

"Henry!" Mrs Whitehead tiptoed down the driveway, sliding past the blue Audi. There was white-hot fury in her voice. "Get away. Let her mourn in peace."

"She's not in," he said again then heard some movement inside the house. He tucked his gut in and straightened his back.

The door opened, and William's mum peered through the gap. Mrs Whitehead gasped then put on the friendliest smile she could muster. "Hello," she said.

William's mum looked at her then at Henry. "Mr Ward?" She had red eyes, her face was swollen, and Henry could smell vodka and cigarettes on her breath.

He jumped in. "Hello there. Myself and Mrs Whitehead here, who's on the parish council, wanted to knock on and see if you were okay."

William's mother looked at him then at Mrs Whitehead and nodded her head slowly.

"Are you doing alright?" Henry asked.

She considered the question for a moment then nodded. "I'm okay."

Mrs Whitehead stepped down the driveway. "Henry here was concerned and wanted me to come with him to see if I can help at all." She spoke as if she was explaining why she was there, but William's mum didn't seem to care.

"Yes, I wanted to know if someone's with you," Henry said.

William's mum shook her head. She seemed to be on the verge of crying and stepped away from the door, hiding herself behind the white panelling.

Henry sensed he was losing her and said, "Look, I'm not sure if the other officers said, but I used to be a detective."

She stopped her retreat behind the door. "Really?"

"Aye, I was a detective in Bradford for forty years."

She stepped towards the threshold and looked at him. "Are you still one?"

He shook his head. "I'm retired. But I've been on many an investigation like this, and I'd like to offer any help I can."

"And I too," interrupted Mrs Whitehead, who was now standing behind Henry at the foot of the doorsteps. "I can get the whole village out helping you, love. There's no need to be alone, not when you've got all of us behind you."

William's mum burst into tears, and Mrs Whitehead barged past Henry to give her a hug.

* * *

The house was minimalist – white walls, dark grey carpets, and not much furniture. What furniture they had looked to be designer, like something from Salt's Mill. Air freshener filled the air with the smell of apple.

There were no pets, and the curtains were drawn and none of the lights were on. Mrs Whitehead was in the kitchen. She'd put the kettle on to boil and was putting glasses in the dishwasher, ignoring William's mum's insistence to leave it.

William's mum was sat on a high stool at the black, granite kitchen counter, watching Mrs Whitehead with disbelief.

Henry stood near the front door with his walking boots on the doormat. He took them off, as the carpets looked clean, and placed them under a radiator next to a pine shoe rack filled with women's shoes, some black high heels and leather sandals, next to young men's shoes, dirty trainers and a scuffed pair of smart ones.

A side table stood by the door. Its top was glass, and it had black, iron legs. Envelopes sat unopened on it next to a white, cordless landline. He picked up one of the envelopes and read the name of the addressee – Mrs Fiona Knight. He noted she was still married, or hadn't changed her title.

He walked along the hallway. There was a staircase that led upstairs. He'd need permission before he could go up there. Framed photos hung opposite the staircase next to a large mirror.

He caught sight of himself in it as he peered at the photos and part of him asked what he was doing. His skin was almost as grey as what was left of his hair. He was retired, wasn't he? Well, he was just making sure that William and his mum got justice. Not that the police wouldn't get them that.

He turned away from the reflection of the old man in the mirror and bottled up his concerns.

The photos showed William and Fiona a few years ago on holiday. The location seemed to be Mediterranean. A restaurant overlooking a bay in the early evening with the red and yellow sunset behind. Both mother and son were suntanned, he was redder than she. Both were smiling and holding cocktails, his arm around hers, and he was a good foot taller than she.

He heard a glass break in the kitchen and Mrs Whitehead telling Fiona that she'd clean it up. He walked into the kitchen to find Mrs Whitehead bending down on the white-tiled floor picking up shards of glass. "Alright?" he asked.

Mrs Whitehead's face was flush. "Yes, just knocked a glass over."

There was a strong smell of vodka emanating from the broken glass. An over-flowing ashtray sat on the kitchen worktop and the air was thick with smoke.

"It's alright, you don't have to clean up," said Fiona. She wiped a stray tear away from her cheek.

"We can leave you alone if you want?" Mrs Whitehead asked.

Fiona considered her question and nodded. Just as Mrs Whitehead was about to concede defeat, however, Fiona shook her head. "No, it's all right. I know you're here to help. I'm just a bit..." She sobbed again, and Mrs Whitehead wrapped her arms around her.

After she'd calmed down, and there were mugs of tea on the clean kitchen worktop, Henry asked, "So, are you married?"

She shook her head but didn't say anything else.

"And what can we call you?" he asked.

She seemed appalled at herself. "God. Sorry, call me Fiona."

"Right, this is Mrs Whitehead," he said, pointing to her.

"Hello," Fiona said.

"Have you heard from the police?"

She shook her head. "They said they'd be around today or tomorrow." She let out a long sigh. "I'm not even sure what to do. What do I have to do?"

"There'll be an investigation, a post-mortem, and then they'll release his body for burial."

Tears were filling her eyes again. "I don't even know what to do. I mean" – she sniffed – "he didn't have funeral plans. He was just a kid."

"How old was he?"

She wiped the tears away with her wrist. "Twenty-one this year."

Henry noted his age. "What did he do? Was he studying something?"

She looked up at him as if unsure why he was asking her that but decided to answer. "He was at uni in Nottingham but dropped out. It wasn't for him. He wanted to get into film-making. It's what his dad did. But it's not that easy to get into."

"So he worked at bars or something?"

She nodded. "A bar in Ilkley. And he did some shifts at the local Tesco."

"Do you know where he was the night before?"

She shook her head. "Not exactly. He might've been working. He often went out afterwards. He might've been with one of his mates. Ryan."

Mrs Whitehead's ears plucked up. "Ryan? Ryan Miller?"

Fiona nodded. "Know him?"

"Well, I know his parents."

"I've not met them," she said, leaning over the counter to grab a pack of Marlboro Gold and the newly cleaned ashtray. "Do you mind?" she asked with a cigarette between her lips.

"It's your house," Henry said.

She lit up and sucked in a drag, then blew it out above their heads. The grey smoke lifted to the white ceiling. "Why is it you're really here, Mr Ward?"

Henry straightened his back and glanced at Mrs Whitehead who flashed a glare at him which said, 'I told you this was a bad idea'.

"Look, Fiona," Henry said, "I found your son on that hill. I feel like I'm involved somewhat, and I know that the police aren't as present as they used to be. I mean, have you heard from your family liaison officer?"

She shook her head and blew out smoke. "They've not mentioned one."

"They should be here now with you, but who knows when they'll eventually turn up?"

She looked down at the white tiles as if realising Henry and Mrs Whitehead had taken up that role without being asked.

"I just want to help if I can. I am an experienced detective, even if I am a little past it." He started coughing. The cigarette smoke had tickled his trachea. He managed to keep the cough under control and said, "But I want your permission before I do anything."

"What are you going to do?"

"I'm going to find out what happened to your son."

"But what about the police?"

"Anything I find will be passed on to them, believe me, and I won't do anything that would jeopardise a conviction." He coughed again. "I know my stuff," he said, spluttering.

Fiona put out the cigarette half-smoked when she realised it was making him cough.

"It'll all be above board, I won't break a law or step over the line in any way. See me, at best, as a private detective that you don't have to pay for. And, at least, someone who can tell you what the police are doing."

She didn't seem to be convinced, so he decided to push it further. "Look, Fiona, we've got a stabbing, and your son was left in a field with no CCTV and no witnesses." He sighed as he didn't want to say what he was about to. "This case could drag on for a while. And after a few weeks with no success, the detectives on it will be put onto other cases where there'll have more chance of a conviction." He could see his words were getting through to her, as she was staring down at the white kitchen tiles. "Now, I'm not saying I can solve this case or anything, but I can make some steady progress. Maybe feed enough information to the police so that they keep on the case."

Fiona stared into the distance as she thought about it. A tear dripped from her eye, and she wiped it off her cheek. "I want to know what happened to him, quickly. I don't know if I'll cope waiting months on end."

He nodded his understanding. He'd seen mums in a similar position to Fiona who hadn't coped with waiting for months, sometimes years, to find out what'd happened to their children. "Alright. I'll go snoop around and let you know what I find."

Her hand jumped out and grabbed his wrist. "Thank you, Mr Ward."

Chapter Nine

They left the house after Mrs Whitehead had promised to come up later in the day with a dish of sausage casserole. She said she'd get the local WI on the case so Fiona wouldn't have to cook for a while. Not that Henry thought she ate much. She had a model's physique and seemed to exist on cigarettes and vodka.

They walked along the pavement through the leafy housing estate. Mrs Whitehead was wittering on about how lovely she thought Fiona was and how she'd done the right thing by going up to make sure she was okay. Henry didn't bother reminding her that she'd been forced into it.

Then Henry stopped walking. He turned and looked up the pavement towards Fiona's house. "There's only the Audi outside," he said. "I wonder if William had a car."

Mrs Whitehead shrugged. "Probably."

"Where is it then?"

"Well, that's something for you to find out."

They carried on walking along the pavement towards the village. There were some fluffy white clouds in the sky, obscuring the sun, and the road was fairly busy with lunchtime traffic.

"So, what is all this?" she asked, her tone having changed.

"What do you mean?" Henry asked, a little too defensively.

"You, a private investigator? You've been retired ten years, your lungs are shot and you've got a bad hip."

"My hip's not too bad."

"Aye, well, I'll take that one back." They carried on walking. "Don't be giving her false hope."

Henry turned to her, feeling exasperated. "Look, I know you've only known me as a retired old fart, but I did use to be a detective chief inspector. I've investigated rapes, murders, burglaries, serial killers…"

"Yes, Henry, you used to be. I used to be a school inspector after having been a teacher for twelve years. But you wouldn't catch me near a classroom these days."

Henry huffed. "You wouldn't survive ten minutes with the kids today."

"That's exactly my point. Someone stabbed that lad and left him for dead. What do you think they'll do with an interfering old fart who can't run anywhere without coughing his lungs up?"

He pulled a grimace and stewed on her words until they made it back into the village. She offered him lunch at one of the pubs. The weather wasn't too cold, and there were a few people sitting at the tables outside the Yorkshire-stone walls of the pub. He declined, however. He wanted to get back and start thinking about the case. Plus, he was still smarting at her words.

"Fine," she said, as they walked towards their houses. "Let me know how you get on or if you need anything."

"Aye," he said, still sulking slightly. "I'll need to chat with that Ryan at some point."

She pulled a face. "Please don't make a fuss with the Millers. They're a nice family, and she's on the parish council."

"Where do they live?"

"That big house behind the pub."

He thought he knew which one she meant. It looked like it'd been built by a small landowner at the turn of the last century. It had a large, walled garden and had been renovated recently, so its top level had a small glass balcony that looked out over the village.

"What do they do, the parents?"

"She's a doctor part-time, and he works in finance or something. He works from the house."

He made a mental note of that and wondered if he knew anyone who could advise him on financial crime.

"Henry!" she snapped, now standing in her front yard and leaning over her fence. "Don't go bothering them. They're a nice couple."

He nodded and opened his own gate and made sure the lock was on when it was closed. "I won't bother them. I'll just be asking their son some questions about the other night." He traipsed along his front yard and took out his front door key.

"Why would he answer any? Under whose authority?"

He opened the door and climbed up his front steps. "You know who. William's mother."

* * *

Henry stood in the kitchen and made some tea. Tessa was hovering around by his feet, and he promised to take her out later. He'd have to go speak to the Millers anyway.

He looked out his kitchen window at his small walled backyard, which he hadn't bothered to weed nor touch for the past year. The whitewashed walls were over six-feet high and backed onto the grounds of a local park. There was an acer tree that had seen better days in a big pot near the wall, next to some others containing brown, shrivelled-up plants that he could no longer identify. He let Tessa out of the back door so she could patrol the yard then took the teabag out of his cup.

He left his cup of tea on the worktop and turned to the round kitchen table near the wall. It was completely covered in letters, magazines, and newspapers, which were stacked nearly a foot high in places. He started clearing them off, sorting out the letters he needed from the ones he didn't. When he was finished, he wiped down the vinyl tablecloth, which was green and had impressionistic ladybirds on. Then he went into the living room and pulled out one of the drawers in the dresser. It was rammed full with old stationery and paper.

Returning to the kitchen table, he placed a crumpled sheet of A3 paper he'd found and started making notes with a black marker.

He wrote down the location of the body – farmland north of the village. Who owned it? Had the owner seen anything? How had William come to find himself there? Had he driven up there or walked? Did he have a car?

He put the date of the murder: Saturday, 12 May, early morning. Where had William been beforehand?

He wrote down William's address and noted down the facts he'd gleamed from Fiona: William worked at a bar – which one? He also worked at Tesco – who knew him there? Was he with Ryan Miller the night he died? What were they doing? What was his home life like? Where was his father, the one who worked in films?

He paused and wondered if the police had William's mobile phone. What would be on it? He knew most cases these days were solved by having techies search the victim's phone for clues. He couldn't remember finding a mobile in William's pocket. If William's phone wasn't on him, where was it? Who had it?

Henry had found the bag of drugs on William and guessed the police were looking into that as a possible angle. He wrote down 'DRUGS' on the sheet of paper. Was William taking them? Who was he getting them off? Was he smoking cannabis or injecting heroin –

there was a big difference.

He recalled the bag of drugs he'd found in William's pocket. It was a white powder, probably cocaine, or possibly something else. If it were cocaine, there was quite a few grams of it in there, based on Henry's rusty summation. That would have cost a bit of money. Where had William got that money from?

Henry took a step back from the table and sipped his tea, which was now lukewarm. The sheet had a lot of questions written on it but not many answers, and he guessed he'd be adding more questions as the investigation went on. But at least an investigation had started.

He was back on the hunt.

Chapter Ten

Henry had a simple lunch, a tuna mayo sandwich, got Tessa on her lead and headed out the front door. Main Street was fairly busy with traffic; numerous four-by-fours drove up and down its narrow lanes. He smiled at a couple whom he recognised from the quizzes he did at the pub. They were a similar age to him and were also out walking their dog, a golden retriever. He didn't stop to chat, mind, as he had a plan.

He crossed Main Street, after waiting for a gap in the traffic, and headed towards the nearest pub, The Fleece. A few diners were sat outside on the large seating area. In summer, all the tables would be jam-packed with people trying to get as much sun as they could. Now, in mid-May, there were only a few tables occupied.

The pub had been in the village since the Civil War, and its facade was shrouded in a sweep of ivy that gave the old building extra character. He smiled at some of the people sat out front then headed down a narrow passageway at the side of the pub.

Tessa sniffed at the weeds along the side of the path, and he pulled her lead so that she'd keep up with him. He came out of the passage and entered a small estate of houses built in the late eighties. He looked at the houses he passed. Most were empty as it was the middle of the afternoon. He wondered if anyone would be in at the Millers' house. If the mum worked part-time then she might be at home, and hadn't Mrs Whitehead said the dad worked from home?

He walked out of the estate and along the pavement that lined the road towards Bolton Abbey. One of the curtains on a nearby house twitched. He often walked Tessa down here, so he wasn't worried about people looking at him. He'd just be some old fogey out walking his dog.

He continued along the pavement and saw the roof of the Millers' home over the tops of some short birch trees. It was a big, Georgian house. In fact, it seemed to have a narrow tower built into it. The new glass balcony jetted out from the top level on a cantilever. Its sleek, glass modernity jarred with the Georgian aesthetic. It must have cost a lot to scar a house like that. The stone walls that surrounded its gardens were lined with some security wire, which had been covertly hidden among some ivy.

Henry stood opposite the house and its walled garden but couldn't see if anyone was in. There was a large wooden gate that needed to be opened manually to get cars out. There must be a driveway and a garage within the walled grounds, he thought. The grounds weren't big, less than a quarter of the size of a football pitch. But that land and the house would have cost a lot. He wondered what it was the Millers' dad did in finance.

A car drove down the road. Realising he'd been staring at the building for too long, he bent down and took out a poop bag from his pocket. He mimed picking up some invisible dog dirt then carried on walking Tessa.

* * *

Henry got back home and let Tessa off her lead. He draped it over the back of his chair in the living room then went to his round kitchen table. He needed to speak to the Millers, but he couldn't do that yet. He'd be better off going with Mrs Whitehead, whom he could use as a pretence. Could he get Ryan to one side while Mrs Whitehead spoke to his mum or dad?

He looked back at his notes on the kitchen table. He wouldn't know if the police had found William's mobile phone, and he wasn't going to ask them if they had. Perhaps he could get Fiona to ask them the question instead. A grieving mother would have lots of questions to ask.

He pored over his notes. There was the drug angle, but he had no idea whom he could ask about that. Henry wasn't part of the Addingham drug world.

There was information that the police had, which he couldn't access. Like William's mobile phone records and his internet history. And there were some questions he had for Fiona to ask them.

The one thing going for him was that he could act more quickly than the police. They still hadn't announced William's name to the press; that was likely to come out the following day. William had probably not even been autopsied yet, as it was a weekend, and that was normally done during the week. Forensic pathologists he used to work with liked to spend their weekends with their families or on the golf course. Well, they did spend their weeks cutting up bodies, so who could blame them?

The proper police investigation wouldn't get going until Monday morning. So, that left Henry today to start looking into things. If he could get to people of interest and shock them with the news of William's demise, he might be able to make some headway before the police made it too difficult for him.

Looking over his notes again, he realised he could investigate William's jobs. They probably wouldn't have heard the news yet. Plus, he needed a few things from the supermarket.

* * *

His six-year-old Skoda Octavia was slightly battered inside. Its seats were covered in Tessa's brown and white dog hair, but it still ran okay. He'd got the car on finance after his previous one had died. He'd decided to buy it outright when the finance had finished as he barely drove anymore and just needed something to get to the shops in.

He parked up in the Tesco car park, in one of the spots reserved for the elderly. Well, he might as well. He searched his glove box for his old Moleskine notebook – the journalists' kind – and a stubby pencil, then got out.

The car park wasn't that busy for a Sunday. The Tesco itself was a squat building, and there was a faint smell of bread coming from somewhere. He headed into the entrance, which was too bright and noisy, and picked up a shopping basket. He pretended to peruse some of the produce, the cherry tomatoes and red peppers, until he found one of the Tesco workers loading up a display of French beans.

He put on his 'dithering old man' persona and toddled up to her. "Hello, love," he said, in as broad a Yorkshire accent as he could manage.

The woman wearing the unflattering, navy blue Tesco uniform stopped loading the French beans and looked at him. "Can I help?" Her expression suggested she'd like to do anything but.

Henry took a deep breath. Either he was going to create a horrendous scene or he was going to get somewhere. "Aye, I'm looking for my grandson," he said, smiling. "He said he worked here."

She straightened up, and he saw her name tag: 'Karen, Deputy Manager'. "Alright. What's he called?"

"William Knight."

She smiled. "Oh, are you William's grandad? Nice to meet you."

He nodded. "Aye, I wondered if he's in?"

"Not today. He doesn't work Sundays."

Henry had guessed right. William's name hadn't been made public yet, so his colleagues at Tesco wouldn't know what had happened to him.

He pretended to be disappointed. "Shame. I thought I'd catch him slacking." He grinned. "Which department does he work in again?"

"Bakery," she said. "From what I hear he doesn't slack much, does Will."

Henry nodded. "Right. I'll go see if I can get some bread. Thanks for your help."

He toddled away from the woman and walked down the aisle with his empty basket.

The bakery section was quiet. There were shelves of oven-baked bread and a glass display of cakes and buns. Henry ignored an urge to buy an iced bun and walked up to a young lad wearing a Tesco uniform.

"Excuse me," he asked, this time in his authoritative police tone.

The lad was loading up one of the shelves with loaves of brown bread. His face was covered in acne, his hair was long and greasy, and he sighed upon seeing Henry. "Can I help?"

Henry spotted the name tag on his dark blue jacket: 'Michael'.

"Is William Knight working today?" he asked.

Michael shook his head. "He doesn't work Sundays."

"Do you work with him?"

A quick nod. He looked a bit out of it. His face was sallow and his eyes were bloodshot.

"Have you heard the news then?"

He shook his head.

"William was found murdered yesterday at the top of Addingham."

The lad's face went paler, and he looked as though he was about to be sick. "You what?"

"Aye, he was found with a stab wound in his back. Police are investigating now. Did you know him well?"

He shook his head. A blatant lie, Henry felt. He'd seen enough of them to know.

"Are you sure you didn't?"

Michael nodded again.

"So, if the police looked on your mobile phone, they wouldn't see a slew of messages between you and him?"

His bloodshot eyes widened further.

"Listen, you can talk to me or you can talk to the police."

He looked at Henry. "You're not the police?"

Henry shook his head. He didn't want to be accused of imitating an officer, so he said, "I'm retired. But I'm working for William's mother to find out what happened to him."

The lad's eyes narrowed as he thought this through. He was probably wondering why this old man was investigating anything.

"Now, as I've already said, you can talk to me or you can talk to the police."

"I don't want to talk to anyone," he said, seeming to find some fighting spirit.

"That's not an option."

"Leave me alone," he said, turning and leaving the tray of fresh loaves of bread on the ground.

He was about to walk into the personnel-only section when Henry said, "Oi, Michael! You either talk to me or I make a fuss and get you fired."

"For what? I haven't done anything."

"You're clearly stoned out of your head, and I can say whatever I like. Do you think Karen, your deputy manager, won't listen to an old codger like me over a druggie like you?"

Chapter Eleven

Michael agreed to speak around the back of the supermarket where the lorries unloaded their goods. High rack trolleys wrapped in sheets of cellophane littered the place as they walked out of the back door. There weren't any other workers around, and Henry guessed there would not be any deliveries on Sundays.

Michael pulled his e-cigarette from his pocket and sucked its nib then let out a plume of blueberry-flavoured vapour. It drifted past him and was carried away on the breeze.

Henry wafted its smell away. "So, tell me about William Knight."

Michael sucked on his e-cigarette again as if he needed it for sustenance. "He's really dead?"

"Aye. I found him. He'd been left on the hill. Were you with him on Friday night?"

He shook his head abruptly.

"Did you see him on Friday night?"

He scratched a spot near his nose as if he was wondering if he could lie to Henry or not.

Henry explained the situation. "Listen, you don't have to tell me the truth. I'm not the police. But if you do lie to me, you'll be putting William's mum through more aggravation, and you'll then be forced to tell the police the truth at a later point anyway."

Michael's eyes narrowed and he sucked on his e-cigarette again. He wasn't convinced.

"He worked in a bar, did William?"

Michael nodded. "He worked at The Platform Edge."

It was a fancy bar in the train station that had been set up a few years ago. Henry hadn't been in but had walked past it a few times.

"Let me guess, he worked Fridays and Saturdays?"

Michael nodded.

"Do you work there?"

Michael didn't respond.

"I can just go and ask them."

He sighed, showing frustration. "No, I don't work there. I just work here."

Henry made a mental note to go to The Platform Edge bar next if it was open. William had been working there the night he died. Had anyone seen anything? Was there CCTV? If there was, how could he get it?

Michael sucked on his e-cigarette and blew out another plume of sickly-sweet-smelling vapour.

"Are you into drugs?" Henry asked.

Michael shook his head. "Not massively."

"Just the odd spliff at work?"

He lifted up his e-cigarette. "I don't smoke spliffs."

Henry realised the cannabis was in the plastic device somewhere. "Ah, that's why you're sucking on that for dear life."

Michael didn't seem amused by his observation.

"Was William into drugs?"

"I'm not... He wasn't that into them."

"But he dabbled?"

He nodded.

"What? Cocaine?"

Michael scrunched up his nose. "No, we don't do that shit."

"Can't afford it?"

"I work here, don't I? What do you think?"

Henry looked at his slightly tattered Tesco uniform. "What do your parents do?"

"Not much. My mum's a social worker, my dad doesn't work anymore. He's on disability."

"Right. And you live with them?"

"Can you afford rent around here?"

Henry doubted he could afford the rent in Ilkley on his fairly generous police pension. He guessed this lad needed this Tesco job pretty badly. It probably helped balance out the family's finances. That was why he had agreed to stand out the back of Tesco and talk to him. "Alright, lad, you won't tell me if you were with William on Friday night?"

He sucked on his e-cigarette and didn't answer.

"Did he have any enemies you know of?"

He looked down at the black tarmac. "Not enemies. Not Will. People liked him."

"Who liked him?"

He looked back up at Henry and said, "Everyone. He was a good lad, was Will." His bloodshot eyes watered slightly, and he shoved the nib of his e-cigarette back in his mouth.

* * *

Henry was glad to get away from that blueberry stink, but he was certain that it'd got stuck on his fleece. He left his car in the Tesco car park and headed to the train station, which was only a short walk away.

The sky was cloudy and a strong breeze was blowing, which rustled what was left of his hair. He hoped it'd blow away the blueberry stink from his fleece. Every now and then, the sky would clear, letting a shard of sunshine down to blind him.

The train station was fairly empty. A few people wearing nice coats stood around nice suitcases waiting for the next train to Leeds. The platform announcement said it'd arrive in fifteen minutes. They were probably heading off back down to London and had been up to see family over the weekend.

He walked along the platform and wondered when he'd last been to Leeds or Bradford. Probably not since he went to see that consultant about his hip, which had been a waste of time. "Let's see how you are in six months' time," he'd said.

The Platform Edge bar was built into the old part of the train station, which had been constructed in the late nineteenth century. Parts of the station had been sold off over the years, and all that was left for its original purpose was the train platforms and a small ticket office.

There was a small seating area out the front of the bar, and large outdoor heaters were mounted on the walls above the seats. The tables were occupied with some drinkers, and the heaters glowed red. Henry felt the wave of heat and thought it was a waste of energy having them on. It wasn't that cold.

The inside of the bar was fairly busy. There was the sound of a football match on somewhere. The interior, inspired by the Victorian period, featured a black bar with a mirrored wall behind it. The seats were organised in booths, like a late-nineteenth-century saloon. There was a strong smell of mint in the air, and Henry saw a young barman making a cocktail.

He walked up to him and looked about the bar. There didn't seem to be anyone waiting to be served. It must be table service, he thought.

"One minute, mate," said the young barman. He wore a denim shirt that had the bar's name on it in black lettering, and was crushing ice and mint with a metal implement. There was no name tag.

Henry waited until he had prepared the drinks then placed them on a circular silver tray, where a colleague – a young woman – collected it from the bar and carried it to one of the booths.

"What can I get you?"

"Did William Knight work here?"

The young lad's eyes widened. "Yeah. He does, why?"

"So, you've not heard?"

The young lad looked completely confused. His steady monotony of making cocktails had been disturbed. "Heard what?"

Henry watched his expression carefully as he said, "He was found dead yesterday morning."

The young lad's cheeks reddened slightly, and his eyes widened further. "You what?!"

"Do you work Friday nights?"

He nodded.

"With William?"

He nodded again. "All night, yeah. Are you the police?"

Henry was about to reply when the young woman returned to the bar carrying the now-empty tray. She leant over the bar to pick up a wet cloth. The barman called out to her. "Have you heard about Will?"

She shook her head and glanced at Henry, wiping the tray in her hand slowly.

"He's dead," the barman said.

She nearly dropped the tray. "What?"

"This guy says he's dead."

"I found him up the top of Addingham yesterday morning," said Henry. He turned back to the barman. "Did you know William well?"

He nodded then shrugged. "I worked with him."

"We all did," said the young woman, who seemed shell-shocked.

Henry glanced at her. The silver tray wobbled in her trembling hand, and she seemed devastated. He wondered if she was a possible girlfriend of William. He looked back at the barman and asked, "What time did you finish on Friday night?"

He'd placed his palms on the top of the bar and was leaning on it for support. "About three. We finish at one, then it's an hour clean-up and then we had some drinks here."

"How did William get home?"

"He drove."

"What car does he have?"

He shrugged as if it wasn't worth thinking about. "Some red Ford Ka or something."

So he did have a car. But where was it now? "He drove despite having had a drink?"

"Yeah. Have you ever seen any police around here?"

He acknowledged that West Yorkshire Police didn't have enough manpower to have officers on country lanes trying to catch drunks when there was routinely hell going on in Bradford and Leeds. "Did you go with him?"

The barman shook his head. "He went off on his own." He looked out the corner of his eyes at the young woman, who was now leaning on the bar for support. He looked back at Henry, his eyes looking slightly angered. "Listen. This isn't a wind-up, is it?"

Henry lifted his hands. "It was on the local news last night, though they didn't announced who'd died. Only his mum, me, and a few people in Addingham know what's happened." This didn't seem to fully appease the barman so Henry asked, "I mean, have you had any contact from William since early Friday morning?"

He shook his head then looked away sullenly.

"Do you have a manager here?"

He nodded. "Around the back. Though, you won't get much sense out of him."

Henry wondered what that meant and left the barman as he started to console the young woman. He decided he'd speak to her later.

There seemed to be something there worth asking questions about.

Chapter Twelve

The corridor to the manager's office looked like something out of a submarine. It was lit by strip lights and wasn't wide enough to fit two people abreast. The walls were bare concrete, unpainted, and there were metal tubes and piping running the length of the low ceiling. The vast sums of money spent on the bar's interior hadn't reached here. Which probably said a lot about how the owners treated their workers. There was also a strong smell of alcohol as if the drainage of the bar ran along one of the pipes.

The door at the end of the corridor was ajar, and Henry knocked on it. Someone said, "Hang on!" Then Henry heard a loud sniff from inside before the person said, "Come in."

The office itself was barely big enough to hold a desk and a banged-up metal filing cabinet. Sat on a leather chair with cuts that exposed its stuffing was a large, bald man. He wore a black T-shirt that stretched around his considerable gut. His face was pale, as if it barely saw the sun, and he had tuffs of stubble on his chin. The man wiped the top of the desk with one hand while the other was brushing his nose. "What?"

Henry cleared his throat to get the man to look at him. When he did, the old man sat back in his chair and pointed back down the corridor. "The gents are down there, mate."

"I'm here about William Knight."

"Alright," said the man, wiping the desktop again. There was a rolled-up twenty pound note next to the computer's keyboard. "What's he done now?"

"He's been stabbed."

The bald man's eyes widened. "Stabbed?"

Henry nodded. "He worked here?"

"'Worked'? So, he's–" His hand covered his unshaven chin. "Bloody hell."

"Are you the manager?" Henry asked, stepping into the office. It smelt of body odour and there was a tint of washing-machine powder, which he guessed was the cocaine.

"Yes," he said, visibly shaken by the news. Either that or he was feeling the cocaine rush through his nervous system. "Are you sure?"

"He's definitely dead. Unfortunately."

He shook his head as if admitting he'd asked a silly question. "When?"

"Early Saturday morning."

"Yesterday?"

"He worked here Friday night?"

"Yes, he worked on the bar. Best cocktail guy I've seen in Ilkley."

"And he left here around 3 a.m.?"

He blew air out of his chubby cheeks. "Possibly. We had drinks after the clean-down. So yeah, possibly."

"You don't remember?"

He shook his head.

"Do you know where he went?"

"He went off on his own, I think."

"You've no idea where?"

The fat man shook his head then snorted his nostril. "Excuse me, hay fever," he said, trying to pretend he hadn't just snorted a line of cocaine.

"What if I told you he was found on the moors outside of Addingham?"

He shrugged. "I'd wonder why he was up on the moors."

"You don't know anything about him outside of work?"

He shook his head. "We all socialise here, the staff, and we know a few things about each other, but we don't know everything."

"I see." Henry looked around the small office. On the desk was a computer screen; on it were some spreadsheets. There was a cork noticeboard on the wall above the computer, and pinned to it were some safety notices and a schedule. "What nights did William work?"

The fat man leant forward towards the noticeboard, his chair squeaking in despair; he read it and said, "Weekends mostly. Rarely worked during the week as he worked elsewhere."

"Did he work with those two out front?"

"Who? Louise and Ben?" He nodded. "Normally did, why?"

"Do they get on?"

He shrugged. "I like to think we all get on well."

Henry couldn't decipher what he meant by that, but it didn't make him feel comfortable. "Do you know if William did drugs?"

The fat man leant back in his chair. "No idea."

"You've never seen him do a line of cocaine or smoke a spliff or anything?"

He shook his head. "Nothing like that happens on these premises."

"Obviously, otherwise your alcohol licence would be in jeopardy."

He cleared his throat and swallowed hard. "Exactly that."

"If I were to search you now, would I find any illegal substances?"

His face went paler. "Are you going to search me?"

Henry shook his head. "I'm not police. So, I don't have the right."

The man's expression changed from fear to frustration in an instant. "Then who the hell are you?!"

"I'm investigating this case for William's mother."

"You're some bloody snoop! Or a journalist?" He wiped his lips with the palm of his hand excitedly. "Is Will even dead?"

"Aye, you can trust me on that. He is very dead."

"Well, I'm not bloody saying another word to you. Get out!"

Henry raised his hands up in submission. He feared the fat man would haul himself out of his chair and start pushing him around. "I'm going. Just make sure you flush your stuff away before the real police call by."

* * *

Henry walked along the bar and glanced at Ben and Louise, the two bar staff. Ben was hugging Louise, who was quietly crying into his denim shirt. Luckily, there wasn't anybody wanting a drink.

Ben looked towards Henry and asked, "Did he tell you anything?"

"Not much," Henry said, stopping near the bar to lean on it. "So, you wouldn't know what happened to William?"

Ben shook his head, and Louise continued crying quietly on his chest.

"Did he have any enemies or did he get in with the wrong crowd?"

Ben looked down at Louise in his arms and said, "I don't know. He was going off the rails a little bit. We were worried about him."

Henry guessed the 'we' referred to Louise more than Ben. She wasn't going to do any talking now as she was still torn up by it. "And you don't know where he went off to after he'd finished here on Friday night?"

Ben looked down at Louise again then back at Henry. "He said he was off to some private party."

"Private party? Do you know where?"

He shook his head.

"Do you know whose party it was?"

He nodded. "Some guy called Freddie."

"Freddie?" Henry hadn't heard anyone called that for a while. "What do you know about him?"

"He's a bit older. Into drugs."

"Like William?"

Louise pulled away from Ben's chest with her eyes red and her make-up smudged. "Alright. Don't say any more," she said.

Ben set his jaw and kept his lips tightly shut.

Henry took his cue to leave and headed towards the doors. Outside, he saw a black BMW cruise along the road, looking to park nearby. He saw the driver in the car had blonde hair. "Shit," he said, under his breath.

He tottered off in the opposite direction before DI Barnes spotted him.

Chapter Thirteen

Henry got back to his Skoda Octavia and sat in the driving seat. The mid-afternoon sky had darkened as if it was about to rain. He heard droplets splat on the windscreen.

He'd managed to keep out of DI Barnes's sight. He was surprised she was out and about on a Sunday. Maybe she was ambitious, or they had a stronger work ethic down south. How would Ben and Louise react when they saw DI Barnes walk in and show them her ID card? They'd probably say, "We've just spoken to one of your lot."

She'd probably come out to speak with him later to give him a bollocking. He wasn't looking forward to that prospect, but he wasn't going to let it stop him. He wasn't doing anything wrong by asking questions, and he'd been clear he wasn't the police, to the best of his knowledge.

He pulled out his Moleskine notebook and stubby pencil from his fleece pocket and started writing up what he'd found out. Possible drugs link. William left The Platform Edge to go to a 'private party' with someone called Freddie. He'd gotten in with the wrong crowd.

He pressed his head against the headrest. His hip was aching slightly as he'd walked away from the bar too quickly. He'd have to have a painkiller later, but not yet, he still needed his wits about him.

William had driven his red Ford Ka to the private party. Unless the police had already found it, there was a chance the car was still sitting somewhere. If it was, Henry could head over to the small hamlet on top of that moor, which looked out over the valley and opposing hills, and find it. Did this Freddie live up there? Had William gone up and then tried to walk down the hill back into the village when something happened to him?

Henry started the engine and decided to head over to Fiona's before going up the tops. He wanted to see how she was doing, and also find out if she had a spare key for William's car, in case he found it.

* * *

Henry knocked on Fiona's front door. Her blue Audi hadn't moved since he'd been that morning. He also saw that there was enough space on the paved driveway to fit another, smaller car.

Fiona opened the door eventually. Her eyes were half closed and her black hair was tied up in a messy bun. "Sorry, Mr Ward. I was asleep."

"Sorry for waking you," Henry said, making to walk down the front steps. "Shall I call tomorrow?"

She shook her head. "No, come in. The police have been."

Henry climbed back up the steps and stepped through the front door.

She lit a cigarette in the kitchen then crushed it out in the already-full ashtray. "Sorry. They make you cough." She was sitting on one of the black stools at the granite kitchen island.

Henry pulled out a stool and sat opposite her. "It's alright. Smoke away."

She considered it then shook her head and pushed the ashtray away from her.

"What did they say?" he asked.

She nodded as she remembered what he was talking about. "They asked me where he worked, if he had a car, if I'd seen his phone."

"Ah," Henry said, glad that he'd already worked out where William had worked and that he had a car. "The phone. Have you seen it?"

She shook her head. Her fingers were held closely to her lips where she picked at a small scab on them. "He had it with him."

"If they asked you where it was, I suspect he no longer had it."

"That'd be odd. He always had it with him. I couldn't get him off it."

Henry didn't want to say that it'd probably been taken by his attacker. "I've been to his places of work."

"Already?" She sounded surprised.

"Yes, I learnt he'd worked Friday night at The Platform Edge bar then finished around 3 a.m., when he apparently left and drove to a 'private party'."

"A private party. Where?"

"I don't know yet. I suspect, if I can find out where his car is, we'll find out where the party was." Unless, whoever had killed William had also taken his car keys and driven it away. Henry suddenly felt glum about his prospects but realised Fiona was looking at him intently, so he put on a brave face. "Do you have a copy of his car key for emergencies?"

She narrowed her eyes as she thought about it and nodded. "Yes, upstairs, I think." She jumped off the stool with some grace then went upstairs.

Henry looked about the kitchen. It must've been renovated a few years previously, as it was all modern and looked top of the range. He then wondered what it was that Fiona did that she could afford an expensive house and car. Saying that, why did her son work two jobs?

She rushed back down the steps and came back into the kitchen. There was a set of car keys in her hand with the Ford logo on them. She placed them on the granite worktop.

"Excellent," he said, "can I take them?"

She nodded. "Of course."

He pocketed the keys and said, "If I find the car, I'll have a look inside and see if there's anything that can help."

"Okay." She sat back on the stool.

"Was there anything else the police said?"

She shook her head. "Not really. They're going to have more information for me in the next few days… and probably more questions."

"That's more than likely."

"I didn't mention anything about you," she said.

"Good. Well, not that they'd be mad at you for that. They'd more than likely have some harsh words for me."

"Why?" she asked, sounding uncertain.

"Police don't like others getting in their way. They're not used to it. But I'm not doing anything illegal. I'm just seeing what I can find out before they can."

She nodded, seemingly more assured. "Right."

"What is it you do, Fiona, if you don't mind me asking?"

She straightened up slightly then said, "I was a dancer, back in the day, for music videos and musicals. Married an up-and-coming director, had William, then we had some problems… The marriage went south, and I left him and brought William up here."

Henry processed what she'd said. "Are you from around here?"

She shook her head. "I'm from South Yorkshire, but I didn't want to live around there, there were too many ghosts. So I came further north. I'd heard it was nice and safe around here to bring up William." She covered her mouth and started weeping on the realisation that it wasn't as safe as she'd thought.

Chapter Fourteen

Henry struggled to get his Skoda Octavia up the narrow country lanes, which were barely wide enough for one car. He was sure he'd already scratched his side of the car against a drystone wall. He continued on, regardless, hoping that no one was coming down the other side, as he didn't know where he could pull in.

He was heading up to the hamlet on the top of the hill. The light rain that had started earlier continued to dribble over the hill and valley. His windscreen wipers couldn't clear it away fast enough.

He thought through the facts of the case again as he drove. William had driven his red Ford Ka onto the moor after he left The Platform Edge around 3 a.m. He was heading to a private party organised by someone called Freddie. Maybe something happened to him at the party, causing him to walk home, down the hill and through its fields, where he collapsed next to a drystone wall. Had he been stabbed beforehand or in the field? Henry would have to figure that one out.

He recalled the scene where he'd found William and realised he'd forgotten something. Wasn't William missing a shoe? Could it still be on the hill somewhere or had someone picked it up?

A car horn startled him, and Henry saw the grilled bumper of a Land Rover rushing down the hill towards him. He pulled his Skoda towards the drystone wall, bumping its side, and leaving just enough space for the Land Rover to pass. He fought the urge to jump out and inspect the damage on the side of his car straightaway. He'd have a look at it later.

The hamlet was a collection of farmhouses, converted barns, and a white modernist house built after the war. They were connected together by a comparatively wider country lane that ran along the spine of the hill.

Henry parked his car near the entrance of a driveway that led to a farmhouse. The rain was still coming down in thick sheets, so he picked up his anorak from the back seat and brushed some of Tessa's hair off it.

He pulled the hood over his head and locked his car. Walking around its side, he went to inspect the damage. It wasn't too bad, just a foot-long scratch next to the left headlight. It would cost a bit to put right if he couldn't live with it.

He looked up and down the country lane before deciding to walk towards the houses. He didn't have Tessa with him; she was at home on the sofa, which denied him his 'dog-walker' cover. He'd just have to pretend he had another reason, should anyone ask, for being up there in the rain. Maybe he was a house buyer?

The first farmhouse looked like it was still a working one. The smell of cow muck came from it, and a Border collie barked at him through the railings of a metal stock gate. He doubted the farmer here would hold a drugs party, and carried on along the lane.

Then he came to the modernist house. It had white concrete walls and full-length windows that looked down over the valley. There wasn't a car parked in its drive, and the house seemed to be empty. He wondered if anyone actually lived here. He'd have to get Mrs Whitehead on the case.

Next there was a squat farmhouse that seemed to have originally been several separate buildings, connected together over time. It was made from wood and red brick and seemed to be ancient. There were Celtic carvings in the woodwork and some of its windows were small circular holes, dating back to a time when sunlight had to be paid for.

He tottered towards the farmhouse and heard dance music coming from inside. The rhythmic drumbeat echoed around its old walls. He heard some chatter as well. Maybe this was where the party had been held?

He made his way to a large wooden gate with a sign on it that read 'Thistle Lodge'. Peering at the gravel courtyard on the other side, he spotted a polished Land Rover parked beside an outbuilding that seemed as old as the rest of the farm. He heard laughter again and suspected this was the place.

He grasped the old, weathered wood of the gate and tried opening it but it was locked. Looking at the farmhouse, he decided he'd best not start breaking and entering without just cause. He couldn't see William's red car anyway.

He made a mental note of Thistle Lodge and told himself he'd be back there soon.

* * *

Henry drove back down the moorside, driving more carefully than he'd done driving up it. The rain was easing off, making conditions a little better, and nothing had driven up the lane as yet.

He'd not found William's car, but something told him that if his phone had been pilfered, so had his car. Lord knows where it could be.

It wasn't a completely wasted journey, as he felt he'd found the location of the party. He'd have to try to get some information on it to see who lived there and learn who this Freddie really was.

He managed to park his car near his cottage, as it wasn't that busy on Main Street at this time of day, and got out. He was still wearing his anorak despite the rain having stopped. The grey clouds had moved on and now the sun was back, shining down on the valley.

He opened his gate and walked into his front yard. The pain in his left hip had gone from an ache to a burn. He'd been doing too much. He slowed his walking pace to a slow hobble, as each step inflamed the joint more.

As he was a few paces from his door, he saw Mrs Whitehead open hers. She wore a light-pink blouse and some smart-looking beige trousers. She stepped out onto her doorstep and looked down at him. "Where've you been?"

"Out and about."

"Well, you've had a visitor. Not twenty minutes ago."

He made it to his door and put his key in the lock. "Let me guess, was it a blonde police detective in a black BMW?"

"I don't know if she was a police detective, but she was blonde, and she looked pretty peeved off. She slammed your garden gate shut so hard it nearly dropped off its hinges."

"That was probably her." He opened his front door and turned to her. "Are you coming in? I can't discuss this on my doorstep."

She rolled her eyes but acquiesced, shutting and locking her own door before walking out of her yard and into his.

Tessa barked at him as he walked inside the living room. She was full of pent-up energy and needed a walk, but he didn't think he could take her on one, not with his hip on fire. He'd need a good sit-down first.

He put the kettle on and let Tessa run around in the backyard. She ran towards the pots that contained brown, lifeless plants, then sniffed some of the puddles left by the rain.

Mrs Whitehead came into his kitchen and looked at the sheet of paper and notes on the kitchen table. "Well, at least it's an improvement on all the junk you had on it before." She leaned over it. "You've got quite a bit on him already."

"I've got even more on him now." He hobbled over to the table and picked up the marker pen. He started writing up the notes on Freddie and the red Ford Ka with Mrs Whitehead watching over his shoulder.

Once he'd finished, he hobbled back to the kitchen top and made two cups of tea.

"I've not been to The Platform Edge," she said. "Is it nice?"

Henry handed her a cup of tea. "It was alright. I didn't think much of the manager."

"Who's that?"

"Some fat bloke with drug issues."

She pulled a face as if she didn't like to think drug issues existed. "Well, I won't be going there in a hurry."

"Have you heard of someone called Freddie?"

"Mercury?" she asked.

"No, someone in the village, or, more precisely, who lives in the hamlet on the top of the moors."

She shook her head. "Not heard of a Freddie. There's a lovely old guy called Fred in the village."

"I know him. It's someone else. Someone younger."

"No idea. I don't really know people up there."

Henry sipped his tea then said, "There's a modern-looking house up there. Big white thing with big windows. Does anyone live in it?"

She shrugged. "I've no idea."

"Can you find out?"

She looked as if she was trying to find a way to say no but nodded instead. "I'll see what I can do." She waited for him to sip more tea then said, "So, that blonde woman, what are you going to do about her?"

"She's a detective. She probably wants me to stop involving myself in all of this."

"Aye, and she might be right."

Henry scoffed. "Listen, I'm not doing anything wrong by asking a few questions on behalf of a grieving mother."

"That's what you think, but imagine if you were still in the police and some old guy was doing the same."

"Oh, I'd tell him to stop or I'd bang him up." He sipped his tea.

"Well, isn't that my point?"

"I couldn't bang him up, though. As he's not really breaking the law, as long as he didn't hide evidence or impersonate a police officer."

"And you're not doing that?"

He shook his head, then remembered he had the spare set of keys for William's car in his pocket. "Look, I think it's important that I do this. Will you either help me to wrap it up more quickly or get off my back?"

She pulled a face then sipped her tea. "Can you wrap it up that quickly?"

He pulled out a wooden chair from under the kitchen table and sat down on it. He winced as he moved his hip. "I hope so. It looks like whoever stabbed him covered their tracks. They've taken his phone and probably his car, too."

She looked down at him, almost matronly. "Look at you. You need to rest up and take care of yourself."

"I'm fine. Listen, I've not felt this alive for years. It's just my hip that's causing me issues. It'll settle down."

She shook her head and looked out the window above the sink into the backyard. Tessa was barking at something out there, probably a bird that had landed in her territory.

"What do you need me to do?" she asked.

"Find out if anyone lives in that modernist house, then ask around to see if anyone knows someone called Freddie."

"Alright," she said then turned to him. "You don't need me to talk to the Millers?"

He'd forgotten about the Millers. There was young Ryan who Fiona thought had been with William on Friday night. "I forgot about them."

She rolled her eyes again. "It's a good job I'm here, isn't it?"

He sipped his tea then said, "Give me a couple of minutes, and we'll go see them."

Chapter Fifteen

They walked together to the Millers' house. The tables outside the pub were filling up again after the patrons had gone inside the avoid the rain.

Tessa pulled on her lead and dragged him down the passageway, and Henry held her back, unable to keep up with her pace. He'd wanted to leave her behind, but she insisted on coming. Besides, he wasn't sure if he'd take her out later in the day.

Mrs Whitehead was at his side. She hadn't said much since they'd left his house. He knew she didn't want to do this but felt duty-bound to do it. Either through loyalty to Henry or because she felt sorry about William and Fiona. Henry didn't want to ask and risk a scene.

Mrs Whitehead said hello to a middle-aged couple whom Henry didn't recognise as they walked along the pavement towards the Millers' house.

Eventually, they came up to its walled garden, and Henry craned his neck to look at the large Georgian house. A woman was sat on the glass balcony on the top level, she was laid back in a sun-chair reading a book. "Is that Mrs Miller?" Henry asked.

Mrs Whitehead nodded. "She's lovely when you get to know her."

Henry wondered what that meant, and they walked to the reinforced gate that blocked off their driveway. Mrs Whitehead pressed a button on the wall, and there was a loud beep followed by the crackle of intercom static. After a few moments, a man came on and said, "Hello."

Mrs Whitehead leant towards the intercom and said, "Hello, Peter. It's Jean."

"Oh, come in."

The gate moved on its own volition, letting Mrs Whitehead and Henry walk down the drive towards the large double garage. The driveway covered most of their plot of land, but there was a small lawn with a delicately carved fountain in its far corner.

Tessa barked and pulled at her lead as she'd seen something worth chasing on the lawn. Henry pulled her to heel and followed Mrs Whitehead towards the porch. Roman-like columns were on either side of the porch and the name 'White Rose Hall' had been carved into the limestone above them.

A man in his early fifties greeted them at the door. He was tanned and looked like he spent a lot of time in a gym. He wore a dark grey T-shirt, some dark chinos, and sandals over black socks. "Hello, Jean," he said smiling at Mrs Whitehead. He then looked at Henry and the dog and frowned.

Mrs Whitehead went to explain. "Peter, this is my neighbour, Mr Ward."

Henry shook Peter Miller's hand.

"He's interested in the parish council, so I wondered if he could chat with you and Becky."

Peter Miller remained polite but was evidently a bit perplexed. "Sure, what exactly does he want to know about the parish council?"

"About security," Henry said. "I'm sure you've heard about the murder on the moor."

Peter's eyes widened. "Why, yes, I heard something on the news this lunchtime. Not sure what happened, though."

Henry gauged his reaction then said, "I'm a former police officer, so Mrs Whitehead thought it might be worth me chatting with a few members of the parish council."

Peter nodded like it was a purely logical thing to do. "Right, of course. Come in."

Henry left Tessa tied up to one of the columns on the porch. He cleaned his shoes on a doormat and followed Mrs Whitehead and Peter Miller into the house.

They walked down a hallway with parquet flooring and past a large living room where the TV played. Henry glanced into the room and he spotted a lad, around William's age, sat on a huge, white leather sofa. The lad had dark, short hair and didn't seem to notice him.

Henry heard Mrs Whitehead talking to Peter Miller further down the hallway and stepped into the living room. "Hello."

The young lad jumped as he realised Henry was there.

"Are you Ryan?"

The lad frowned. He had black, bushy eyebrows that made his expression look quite hostile. "Yes. Who are you?"

"I'm a friend of your parents."

Ryan nodded his head slightly as if he didn't think that meant anything.

He heard Mrs Whitehead calling down the hallway. "Henry?"

Henry looked to her then said to Ryan, "Got to go." He left Ryan in the living room and traipsed down the hallway.

He'd found his person of interest. Now all he had to do was find a way to talk to him without upsetting his parents.

* * *

Henry continued walking down the hallway and caught up with Mrs Whitehead. She gave him a nasty frown and shook her head. "Not yet," she said under her breath.

They walked past a sweeping staircase that had the same parquet flooring as the hallway, and saw the woman who'd been on the balcony walking down the steps. She had Ryan's dark hair and bushy, hostile eyebrows. "Jean, how are you?" Her tone of voice was almost masculine. She was slim and short, but had an aura around her that made her presence seem to fill the space.

"I'm alright, and you?"

"I was fine, reading a book. What can we do for you?" She walked down to the bottom step and looked at Henry with some curiosity.

Mrs Whitehead was about to introduce Henry to Becky Miller when Henry said, "I wanted to talk to some people involved with the parish council about the murder. To prepare you for what you might expect to happen. What with the media and the police investigation."

Becky Miller's eyes widened, just as her husband's had, then she looked him up and down. "Alright, but what experience do you have with all that?"

"I'm a retired chief inspector."

She seemed impressed and gestured to a doorway that Henry could see belonged to a kitchen. "Let's go and chat, then."

They were provided with coffee that Peter Miller made with an espresso machine built into one of the kitchen cabinets, filling the air with the smell of fresh coffee.

The kitchen was modern but looked old-fashioned at the same time. There was still a large fireplace that was now filled in and had an intricate stained-glass mural of a piece of art that Henry thought had been done by Andy Warhol. A large kitchen island with an oak worktop filled the middle of the room, and all of the gadgets and appliances in the kitchen seemed to be brand new and of the highest quality.

Henry, Mrs Whitehead, and Becky Miller were sitting around the large kitchen island. Peter Miller excused himself, explaining he had work to do in his office upstairs. After he went, Becky Miller said, "He works every day of the week, even Sundays."

"What does he do?" Henry asked, innocently.

"He's into FX trading."

Henry wondered if there was a huge need for foreign exchange traders in Yorkshire as he sipped his coffee. He instantly felt a rush from the caffeine.

"So," Becky Miller said, "what is it we can expect to happen?"

"Well, the police investigation is just getting started," Henry said, feeling his heart beat in his chest. "It'll kick into full drive tomorrow. As they don't have a suspect, they'll be looking for people with any connection to William Knight."

"Oh, it was William?" Becky's cool and collected aura came undone for a few seconds. She absent-mindedly looked through the door and into the hallway.

"Yes," Henry said. "It was William Knight. It'll probably be made public tonight."

Becky Miller looked back at him then at Mrs Whitehead. "How do you two know it was him?"

"Henry found him," Mrs Whitehead explained.

"Where?"

"In a field to the north of Addingham," Henry said. Then he continued, "As I was saying, the police will be speaking to all of William's contacts, getting a picture of what he was like. Then, they'll follow any lines of inquiry that come up." He sipped his coffee again. "As he was found murdered and there isn't any clear indication as to who did it, it could take a while, which might have implications on the village."

Becky Miller didn't seem to be enjoying what she was hearing. "What kind of implications?"

"The longer the investigation the more restless people get. Journalists will be sniffing around, so will busybodies and so on." He thought he heard Mrs Whitehead snigger under her breath as he said 'busybodies' but chose to ignore her.

"Right," Becky said, staring into space.

"Did you know him?" Henry asked.

She came to and locked her dark, brown eyes on his. "Yes, I knew him. He was a friend of Ryan's."

Henry looked at Mrs Whitehead and said, "Who's Ryan?"

"He's my son," Becky Miller said.

"Ah, well. I'd expect the police will want to talk to him at some point."

She nodded curtly then looked down at the oak kitchen worktop. "Yes. They probably will."

Henry took his chance. "Might it be worth me talking to him beforehand?"

She frowned. "Why?"

"I could prep him for any police interview he might have."

"Why would my son need to be prepped for anything?"

"The police will be desperate. They'll be looking for someone to drag into this," Henry said, feeling as though he was blowing his chance.

Beck Miller shook her head. "We don't know if they'll even interview him."

"Did he hang around with William a lot?"

She nodded.

"Becky," Mrs Whitehead said, "I've known Henry since he moved back to the village ten years ago. If he can help, he will. He only means well."

Becky Miller lowered her shoulders and said, "Alright."

"Well, let's get it over and done with while I'm here," Henry said, trying not to betray his desperation to speak with Ryan.

Becky seemed slightly put out but stood up from the table anyway. "I'll go fetch him."

She went out through the door, and Henry sighed. He unzipped the top of his fleece as the kitchen was warm and the coffee had quickened his heart rate. He turned to Mrs Whitehead, "Thanks."

"Don't mess this up," she said, her steely eyes rested on him a moment before she turned away from him.

Shortly after, Becky came back into the kitchen. "We'll have to do it another time."

"Why?" Henry said.

"He's not here. He's gone out somewhere."

Henry looked at Mrs Whitehead, and they both seemed to share the same thought. Ryan Miller had ran off, which made him look like he had something to hide.

Chapter Sixteen

Henry and Mrs Whitehead walked back along the pavement towards their cottages. A few cars drove past whose passengers must have spent the day at Bolton Abbey further down the road.

Mrs Whitehead had to raise her voice to be heard over them as they passed by. "She'll ring you when Ryan comes back."

"Hmm." Henry pulled Tessa back as she was tugging hard on her lead. He didn't think Becky Miller would ring. He felt like he'd blown his only chance.

"Maybe he went out innocently? Went off to meet a friend or something?"

"No, I must have scared him," he said, pulling Tessa away from some weeds she was smelling at the side of the pavement. He knew that once you became a police officer, you had that demeanour about you for the rest of your life. "Do you know what kind of car he's got?"

She shook her head. "No idea. Why didn't you ask?"

He sighed under his breath. "I didn't want to push it with Becky Miller. She seemed like someone who'd rather call in the lawyers and let them deal with it."

"Aye, she probably is. She's usually asking the parish council to call in the solicitors whenever we have a problem."

"Who is she, anyway?"

"Becky? She grew up in the village. That's her parents' house, in fact; but she moved down to London after she finished university. She came back up north and moved into the house after her parents passed away."

"Right, so Ryan didn't grow up in the village?"

She shook her head. "He didn't go to any of the schools, no. He probably went to some private one down south."

"What does he do?"

She seemed to think about it for a moment then said, "You know, I don't think she's ever said."

"Probably spends his days laying about and spending his parents' money," he said under his breath.

Henry wondered what the real reason was for Ryan's departure as they walked down the passageway towards the pub. It was late afternoon, and the patrons on the tables outside the pub had multiplied, but the grey overcast sky threatened rain at any moment.

"Fancy that drink I promised?" he asked Mrs Whitehead, hoping that she'd take it as a 'thank you' for putting herself out on a limb with the Millers.

"I thought it was lunch you promised. Besides" – Mrs Whitehead pointed down Main Street to their cottages where a black BMW was parked outside Henry's – "isn't that your blonde police detective?"

Henry's stomach dropped. "Yes, I think it is."

* * *

Mrs Whitehead left Henry's side as if she didn't know him and walked off in the other direction. He took a breath and walked towards his cottage to face his reckoning. The overcast heavens opened, and water fell down on him and Main Street's tarmac as he crossed it. He heard the patrons outside the pub announce their displeasure at the rain and rush inside.

He quickened his pace and went to his front gate, passing the front of the black BMW. He didn't look inside.

As he opened the front door and ushered Tessa into his house, he heard DI Barnes. "Mr Ward." He turned and saw her at his front gate, umbrella up, and wearing a long navy raincoat. "Can I come in?"

She declined his offer of tea and asked him to sit down. He thought about disobeying her, but that would only make things worse. Besides, he had all his case notes laid out on the kitchen table. He'd have to keep her out of there at all costs.

He took the sofa and let her sit in his green velvet chair. She kept her damp raincoat on and had left her wet umbrella by the front door.

Tessa sniffed her boots then went off and hid around the side of the sofa.

"I've had a strange conversation several times today, Mr Ward."

"Alright," Henry said. "Are you sure you don't want tea?"

"I won't be here long." She looked tired. Her blue eyes were less vibrant than they'd been the day before. A few droplets of rainwater ran down her short blonde hair. "You see, I've been looking into the murder of William Knight, and wherever I seem to go, I'm told that there's been this old detective there before me."

Henry nodded as if it was news to him but didn't say anything.

"I asked who this detective was, and they tell me it's an old guy, wearing a beige fleece; slightly balding with grey hair." Her blue eyes flashed an instant as she looked at him. "Wouldn't you say that's a good description of you?"

"Possibly," he said.

"Now, I can do either of the following. I can take you down to the station and charge you with interfering in a police investigation, impersonating an officer, and perverting the course of justice. I feel I have enough evidence to push for all three charges."

He knew she was only trying to scare him but hated to admit it was working.

"Or I can give you a stern and final warning to desist any further interference in this case, which you will acknowledge and abide by." She tilted her head slightly like she was talking to a child. "So, which is it you want me to do?"

He took a breath to steady his nerves and said, "I'm not doing anything wrong."

"I believe you are. I believe I have enough evidence to charge you, and I suppose it's up to you if you want to see if the courts agree. It's no skin off my nose." Her blue eyes flashed again. "If anything, it'll help me chalk up more charges for the month."

He looked down at his hands which had been on his lap but were now trembling. She saw them and smiled slightly. He forced himself to steady them and said, "What if I give you what I have?"

"You will give me what you have in either instance. That, you have no choice over."

"What if you don't solve his murder?"

She shook her head. "I don't know what it was like back in your day, Mr Ward, but we're under a lot more pressure to solve these types of crimes, and we have a lot more resources to do it with."

"You don't have his phone. You don't have his car. There's hardly going to be any evidence on his body as it'd rained that night, if I remember correctly."

The corner of her mouth twitched, undermining some of her self-confidence. "It's early days, but we're making progress."

"Really? It seems you're two steps behind me."

She sat back in her chair. "Let me remind you of your choices."

"And let me remind you that I'm not doing anything wrong. I haven't imitated a police officer. I've been clear with everyone that I'm a retired police detective working on behalf of the victim's mother."

She tutted and shook her head. "You've manipulated Fiona Knight into letting you do this?"

"I've got further than you have in this investigation."

"Why? What have you found out?"

He was about to tell her then held back. Whatever he told her she'd take and roll with, and no doubt she'd get all the glory. But was he doing this for glory or to find out what happened to William?

"Well," she said, taking his silence as an answer, "it seems you've not got as much as you thought. And, by the way, I have a witness statement from a member of staff at The Platform Edge who said you didn't tell him you were retired. You led him to believe you were an active police detective."

"I did not!" he said, assuming she was lying.

She shook her head and pulled out her mobile phone from the inside pocket of her navy-blue raincoat. She tapped on its screen then placed it down on the arm of the seat.

A voice came out of the speakers and said, "He didn't say he wasn't police. He said he was looking into Will's murder." In the background was chatter and the banging of glasses.

Henry placed the voice as Ben from The Platform Edge, the fair-haired barman. He was pretty sure he'd told him he was retired but maybe he hadn't. He felt self-doubt swell around him.

He heard DI Barnes in the recording ask, "Did he show you any ID?"

"No, he just said he was looking into the murder. He didn't say he was retired or anything."

She stopped the recording and picked up her phone. "So that's what I have on you, Mr Ward." She slid the mobile phone into her inside pocket and looked at him. "Let's call this your final warning, shall we? If I hear anything else, I'll come back here and make an arrest."

"Alright, you do that. I'm sure the courts will realise I've done nothing wrong."

She smiled slightly. "Well, if you're willing to take that risk, I can just arrest you now."

He sat back against the sofa's cushion. "You can leave now."

She stood up, still smiling slightly, and made her way to the front door. "I very much hope this is the last time I see you, Mr Ward. I'm a serious person and once I've made a threat, I make sure I carry it through."

Chapter Seventeen

The living room smelt of DI Barnes's perfume long after she'd gone. He'd stayed on the sofa but then got up and hobbled over to the dresser where he searched its drawers for a painkiller. After he swallowed two without water, he went back to the sofa and sat down, waiting for the pills to kick in.

His heart rate was still high, and he was still breathing like he'd just been for a jog. If he could see his face, he was sure it'd be blotchy. He was grateful his asthma hadn't joined the party.

He rested his head against a cushion and listened to the rain fall outside the window. He could see the grey sky through the blinds. People on the pavement kept dashing past, either on their way to the shop down the street or home.

He wasn't afraid of DI Barnes's threats, but he didn't fancy having to defend himself in court. That's if he ever ended up there. It could take years to get a court hearing these days.

He was more worried about provoking suspicion into his past behaviours. As DI Barnes had said on her last visit, the inquiries only ended because he'd retired. He avoided public humiliation and any serious punishment. Not that he'd done anything as bad as the others who worked under him. He hadn't been involved in organised crime or anything like that. Nothing that could be seen as doing wrong.

But he had pretended not to see stuff, he had avoided asking questions, he hadn't raised any of his concerns with the appropriate people. And he had been rewarded for doing so. Envelopes of cash had been left in his car or in the desk drawer in his office at the station, and there were a few hiding places where he'd stashed it. It wasn't a life-changing amount, but enough to know he could weather a rainy day if needed. He wasn't sure if all of the notes were still legal tender, as some of them were over twenty years old. And he didn't fancy going into the local post office with a bunch of them to find out.

He chuckled to himself. That'd be typical. Feeling guilty about receiving cash he couldn't spend anymore. He licked the side of his lips and looked over at the dresser where the bottle of whisky was. He shook his head. It was still daylight outside, and he still had stuff to do with the case; not that his mind would be as sharp after the pills he'd taken.

He relaxed in the chair and felt fuzzy warmth come over him. Most likely from the opioids. Was he going to continue with the case? Well, he could take DI Barnes's warning and keep out of it. But then what would he do? He'd be on the sidelines watching.

And what about Fiona Knight? He'd promised her answers.

He shook his head at the thought of giving up the case. No, he'd carry on. He'd ignore DI Barnes's warning, and if she wanted to arrest him, she'd quickly find out that going after a retired detective chief inspector wasn't the easiest of things to do.

* * *

Henry must've dozed off. He came to in his darkened living room. The sky outside had turned to late evening, and the street lights had come on, shining an amber glow through his window, cut into strips by the blind.

Tessa was curled up next to him on the sofa, asleep. His phone in his pocket rang, vibrating on his leg. He guessed it'd already rung, as he vaguely remembered hearing it while he was asleep.

He pulled it out of his pocket, which disrupted Tessa, who opened her eyes and yawned. Henry answered his phone. "Hello?"

"Hello, is that Mr Ward?"

Henry cleared his throat, as his voice sounded weak and tired like he'd just woken up. "Yes."

"It's Becky Miller. I just wanted to let you know Ryan's here if you want to speak with him."

Henry flustered about the sofa, trying to get himself up. "Aye, when can I come around?"

"He's staying here for dinner but wants to go out after. I've told him he can't go until he speaks with you. So, as soon as you can, really."

"Right, that's great. I'm on my way."

* * *

Henry pressed the intercom that he'd watched Mrs Whitehead press earlier. Its metal casing was covered with droplets of rain. It beeped after he'd announced himself to Peter Miller, and the gate opened.

He walked along the gravel driveway, the lawn and fountain in the corner were lit by low-level lighting hidden inconspicuously in the bushes. The water of the fountain splashed in its pool.

Peter Miller opened the front door under the Roman-style porch, and welcomed Henry into the house. Henry wiped some of the wetness from his shoes on the doormat, while Peter Miller told him not to bother. He wondered if Peter would take his anorak from him, but he didn't. Henry took it off and folded it over his forearm, noticing some droplets drip onto the floor.

He followed Peter down the hallway, with its brightly lit white walls and high ceiling, passed the living room, and went into the kitchen.

There was a strong smell of garlic in the air, and Becky Miller stood in front of a mint-green Aga cooker stirring vegetables in a wok. A blue and white tea towel hung over her shoulder. She looked up at Henry and nodded. "I'll go fetch him."

"Oh, you've not eaten?" he asked.

She shook her head. "Would you like any?"

Henry felt the invitation was perfunctory and said, "No, thank you. I've already eaten."

She left him alone in the kitchen and shouted for Ryan. Henry walked towards the kitchen island and sat down on one of its red leather stools.

Becky rushed back in and said Ryan was coming. After a few minutes, when Henry wasn't sure if he was actually going to come, Ryan walked into the kitchen.

Henry watched him enter. He looked like he didn't want to be there. His hostile frown was out, and he looked at Henry like he was a piece of excrement.

Ryan walked to his mother at the Aga and asked, "Do I have to?"

She answered with a glare that made even Henry feel uncomfortable.

Ryan stepped towards the kitchen island and sat down opposite Henry. Henry looked over the lad's face. It was pale, his eyes were red and bloodshot, he had stubble on his chin, and a long fringe. He had the same dark hair as his mother. Henry guessed he'd be about the same age as William had been, but wasn't sure. "Hello, Ryan. I'm Henry Ward."

Ryan didn't say anything. In the background, Becky stirred their dinner, pretending she wasn't listening.

Henry looked back to Ryan and said, "I'm a former police detective, a chief inspector."

Ryan was staring down at a knot in the oak worktop of the kitchen island.

"So, how old are you, Ryan?"

He looked up at Henry, his bloodshot eyes looking over him, and said, "I'm twenty."

"And what is it you do?" Henry asked.

He shrugged. "This and that."

Henry noted his accent had a hint of Yorkshire in it, but it was mostly a southern one. He suspected the tint of Yorkshire was put on. "Right. And did you know William Knight?"

He nodded.

"Were you close friends with him?"

He shook his head. "I knew of him, mostly."

Becky Miller slammed a metal spoon onto the kitchen worktop, which made Ryan jump.

"Well, I knew him fairly well," he said, correcting himself.

Henry glanced at Becky then back to Ryan. "Listen, Ryan, I'm not a police detective anymore. But I think I know what questions they'll ask you. It's best that you're honest with me, so I can better advise you on what to say."

Ryan seemed slightly interested for the first time.

"You'll have to tell me the whole truth. If you hold anything back from me, then go on to lie to the police, they'll probably find out and charge you with something else."

Henry glanced over at Becky who was no longer pretending to listen. She was watching the proceedings while leaning against one of the worktops. "Hear that, Ryan?" she asked.

Ryan turned back to her and waved his hand as if to tell her to get lost. Turning back to Henry he said, "I was friends with Will. I knew him since we moved here."

"When did you move here?"

He sighed. "Three years ago."

"Where had you lived before?"

"North London."

"It was a bit of a change, I imagine, moving up here?"

He nodded.

"Did you like the change?"

He looked down at the oak tabletop. "It was important for Mum that we moved back."

Henry glanced at Becky who'd carried on preparing dinner. He wondered what that meant but decided to leave it for another day. "So, you met William three years ago?"

Ryan nodded.

"What was William like?"

"Nice. Everyone liked him."

"Do you know if he had any enemies or people who didn't like him?"

He shook his head. "Everyone liked Will. That's why I was really shocked when I learned what'd happened."

"Right, when did you hear about it?"

His bloodshot eyes looked at Henry. "This afternoon when Mum told me."

"How did you feel?"

He showed that hostile frown. "Like I said, I was upset."

Henry wondered if Ryan's eyes were bloodshot because he'd been crying, or because he'd been smoking something. He'd seen enough cannabis users in his time to make an educated guess. "When did you last see William?"

"I saw Will on Thursday night."

"Oh," Henry said, arching his eyebrows. "Mrs Knight, William's mother, believed you were with William on Friday night."

Becky Miller raised her head from cutting yellow peppers and stared at Henry.

Ryan shifted in his seat. "I wasn't with him Friday night."

"Now, Ryan, the police are quite sophisticated these days. If you were with William on Friday night and you had your phone on you, they can track your movements by looking at your phone's data. Unless, you didn't have it with you, of course?"

His eyes widened, but he didn't say anything.

"Now, do you always have your phone on you?"

He nodded unwillingly.

"Right, so if the police traced your movements by using your phone, do you think they would find you were at the same place as William on Friday night?"

He looked down at the tabletop and started scratching his thumbnail with his index finger.

"Ryan?"

He nodded. "I was with him on Friday night."

"Right," Henry said, feeling excitement build in his gut. "And where were you?"

Ryan sighed. "Up on the moors. At a house party."

Chapter Eighteen

The smell of garlic and soy sauce was getting stronger, but Henry was too excited to think about food. He leaned over the oak tabletop, his elbows resting on it, and cradled his chin in his hand. "Where was the house party?"

Ryan shrugged. "I don't know."

"Had you been there before?"

He shook his head.

"Do you know whose house it was?"

Ryan continued to scratch his thumbnail with his finger. "No. Just heard it was some guy called Freddie."

Henry felt his cheek twitch. He was getting close to something, but he wasn't quite sure what. "Have you met Freddie?"

He nodded.

"What does he look like?"

He shrugged. "Blonde. Quite tall. He's old. Like, thirty or forty."

"What does he do?"

"He says he's a DJ, but he runs some business or something."

"Is he local?"

He nodded. "Yeah, he's from around here. He said he's from Leeds."

"How did you get to the party? It's not easy getting up there."

He shrugged as if he couldn't remember. "It was a taxi, or maybe Will drove, I can't remember."

"Where did you meet William?"

"In Addingham. I'd been at a party here, one of my mates', then Will picked me up." He nodded like he was remembering. "He drove. There were three of us."

"Three?"

"Me, Will, and Louise."

"Louise? Isn't she someone William worked with?"

He nodded.

"At the party, who did you spend your time with?"

Ryan shrugged again. "I've no idea. I was out of it."

Becky Miller tutted in the far corner of the kitchen, where she was leaning against one of the worktops, listening.

Ryan seemed to remember she was there and straightened up in his chair.

"Did anything happen at the party?" Henry asked.

Ryan shook his head.

"How did you get home?"

"I think I called an Uber around nine in the morning. I was still awake but wanted to get home and sleep in my own bed."

"Can you prove you got a taxi? In case the police ask?"

Ryan looked at him like it was a stupid question. "It was an Uber, there'll be proof on the app."

Henry nodded as if he already knew that. "Was William still at the party when you left?" Henry asked, but he already knew the answer to this, as he'd found William's body just before 10 a.m.

Ryan shrugged. "Don't think so."

"You hadn't seen him throughout the party?"

He shrugged. "As I said, I can't remember much."

Henry looked into his bloodshot eyes and wondered if he could believe him or not. Then he changed tack. "What about Louise, did she leave the party with you?"

He shook his head. "I left on my own."

"Oh, what happened to her?"

"She stayed, I think." He looked down at the tabletop.

"Were she and William together or anything?"

"I don't know." He shrugged. "You'll have to ask her about that."

Henry decided he would. "So, between you entering the party with William and you leaving, you can't say at what point William left?"

He seemed to give it some thought, then he shook his head like it was a sum too difficult for him to work out. "No idea."

"You didn't hear any arguments or see a fight or anything?" Henry asked, over the banging of pans. Becky Miller seemed to be getting impatient.

Ryan shook his head and turned to his mum who was walking towards them. "Well," she said, "I think that's enough questions." She smiled at Henry. "Mr Ward, thanks for coming over at such short notice. I think Ryan's fully prepped now. Are you sure you don't want to stay for dinner?"

He declined her offer and rose from the red stool. The back of his legs ached as he stood. He said goodbye to Ryan who quickly skulked upstairs, and Becky Miller walked with him down the hallway to the front door.

"So, do you think he'll be okay?" she asked.

Henry nodded but said, "I think he'd be wise to remember what happened at that party if he can. The police will want to know. And as I said, if he lies to them or holds something back, they'll find out and make him pay."

Becky's face darkened a moment. "I'll make sure he has a solicitor with him."

"No," Henry said, shaking his head. "That would make him look guilty."

She frowned. "He's not guilty. I'm just making sure he has someone to defend him."

"People who need defending usually have something to feel guilty about."

They came to the wooden front door, and Becky Miller opened it for Henry.

"If he remembers anything, you have my number," he said.

She seemed to think on his words a moment then said, "I'll ring you if he says anything else." As Henry was on the front step, she added, "Thank you, Mr Ward. I hope we'll find out what happened to William."

Henry nodded. "I'm sure we will."

* * *

Henry traipsed along the pavement, walking under the amber glows of the street lights as the rain patted on the hood of his anorak. A car drove past slowly then continued onto Main Street and turned left. He watched it go then lost himself in his thoughts.

Ryan had seen Freddie and could confirm the location of the party. Louise had also been there. But, if that was the case, why had she been surprised when she learned that William had been stabbed?

The air smelled of damp stone and grass as he walked down the passageway, heading towards the pub. There were no street lamps down here, so he used the distant lights of the pub to guide him. The alleyway ran down between the backs of two housing estates, one older than the other. It had six-foot-high reinforced concrete walls on either side and led into the pub's car park.

Henry kept one hand near the wall to steady him in the darkness. He returned to his thoughts.

Ryan had said Freddie was a DJ and a business owner. Could Henry find out more by looking at Companies

House records to see if any of his businesses were listed? He could use the name of the house he'd seen on the moors: Thistle Lodge. Not that Freddie was a suspect, but the host of a party at which one of its guests was murdered was worth talking to.

He was nearing the end of the alley when he heard the footsteps of someone walking down behind him. He slowed his pace and turned to find out who it was but only saw a darkened figure.

The figure was walking quickly towards him with something large moving at its side. Henry tottered back around and started walking towards the pub; at least he'd make it to its car park and be nearer to help if he needed it.

As he stepped into the pub's car park, the figure brushed past his shoulder, and in the light from the back of the pub, he saw it was a young lad walking a golden retriever. The lad had big red headphones on his head and was listening to music, completely oblivious to Henry.

Henry took a breath to steady his nerves. His chest felt like it had ballooned in size, so he stopped walking. He'd never got spooked like that before.

He was traversing the pub car park, which was mostly empty. He was dodging the large puddles that covered the tarmac when he felt a shove on his side.

He lost his footing and went down, managing to land on his good hip.

He felt bewildered and looked about and saw a tall, young lad standing over him. He recognised him as Ben from The Platform Edge. He was wearing a black coat and stood over Henry, his finger pointing in his face. "You lied to me!"

Henry rolled off his shoulder and onto his back, landing in a puddle. He felt water run up the inside of the anorak.

"You fucking lied to me! I thought you were the police!"

Henry held up his hands to defend himself from the pointing finger. "I'm retired."

"You still lied to me!"

"Oi," Henry said, getting angry, "you've just pushed over a senior citizen. Either help me up or back off."

Ben snarled at him then took a step back and walked towards one of the parked cars.

Henry sat up and eventually hauled himself onto his feet. He looked over at Ben after he'd wiped some of the water off the back of his anorak. "Now, what the hell is this about?"

Ben looked at him. In the nearby light of the pub, Henry could see a flash of guilt in his eyes.

But guilt for what, he wasn't sure.

* * *

Ben calmed down but declined Henry's offer of going into the pub for a drink. They remained in the car park, standing under an overhanging roof at the side of the pub. The rain had eased but still fell, landing on the tarmac with a whispered splash.

A few patrons from the pub walked out of the back door and crossed the car park, not paying Henry or Ben any mind.

Henry's shoulder hurt from where he'd landed on the tarmac, and his jeans and the inside of his anorak were sodden. But he was determined to get to the bottom of this. "So, what is it that's got you so worked up?"

Ben was smoking a real cigarette, not one of those plastic ones. He blew out the smoke and stared down at a puddle in front of him. "I just panicked and felt angry."

"Right. They're two different emotions. Why did you feel angry?"

He sniffed. "I just felt like you lied to me."

Henry put a hand on his own chest, touching his wet anorak, and said, "I'm very sorry about that. I thought I'd said I was retired. I've told everyone else."

Ben glanced at him from the corner of his eyes, but his expression didn't lighten up.

"Look, I'm not doing this for my own benefit, lad. I'm trying to find out what happened to William for his mum's sake." Henry watched Ben carefully to see if his words were having an affect. "I mean, can you imagine your mum going through the same thing? Would you want her to know what had gone on?"

Ben nodded and looked back at the puddle and smoked. His fair hair was just as wet as Henry's anorak, and his black coat was dripping.

"So, why did you panic?"

Ben turned to him. "What?"

"You said you panicked? What about?"

Ben shook his head. "It's nothing."

Henry nodded as if he agreed it was nothing, then waited a moment before asking, "Is it because you mentioned Freddie's name?"

Ben's eyes widened then he shook his head. "I didn't mention any name."

"You did. You said his name back in the bar. You said William had fallen in with the wrong crowd and that he'd been to someone's party. That someone was Freddie."

Ben clenched his jaw, looked down at the rest of his cigarette, then tossed it into the puddle where it hissed.

"You're not the only one to say his name to me."

Ben looked at him. "That blonde detective said you're not to talk to people."

"That 'blonde detective' says lots of things. Who is he? Who's Freddie?"

Ben looked at the back door of the pub. No one was walking through. "He's some older guy."

"A DJ, I've heard."

Ben nodded. "He's got a house up on the hill above Addingham."

"Thistle Lodge?"

Ben's eyes widened. "Do you know him?" he asked, with a hint of fear in his voice as if Henry had been sent to spy on Freddie's behalf.

"No," Henry said. "Trust me. I don't hang around with drug dealers and the like."

"I didn't say he was a drug dealer."

"Are you sure? It looks suspicious, doesn't it? He holds big parties at his house, the local kids who go up seem to be on something, then one of those kids winds up dead."

Ben didn't say anything.

"Have you been to his house?"

He nodded.

"Were you there on Friday night?"

He shook his head so vigorously Henry believed him.

"Why not?"

"They're crazy. His parties. Out of control."

"Because of all the drugs?"

Ben looked at him almost shamefully and nodded.

"So, people go to the party, get their drugs there, take them, and they get out of control? And you're telling me that Freddie isn't a drug dealer?"

"Sod this!" Ben stepped out from under the overhanging roof and walked through the puddle. He pulled his shoulders up as the rain fell down on him.

"Where are you going?" Henry called out.

He didn't answer and walked onto Main Street where he headed off into the darkness.

Chapter Nineteen

The sky was grey and overcast again, promising another hit-and-miss day. Henry stepped away from the kitchen window. His good hip and shoulder were still smarting from his fall in the car park last night. He still wasn't sure what he was going to do about that. It didn't seem worth pressing charges against Ben. He seemed like a good enough kid really. He'd just gotten in with the wrong crowd, much like William had.

He started the kettle and looked at the kitchen table. The notes he'd made before bed were scrawled around the edges of the A3 piece of paper, as he'd been running out of space. He saw Companies House scribbled on the paper and decided he'd have a look after breakfast.

He put some dry food in Tessa's bowl and looked out at his backyard. The acer tree was looking greener and more vibrant thanks to the rain. If the weather carried on like this, even the dead brown things in the pots next to it might spring back to life.

He hobbled into the living room, switched on the TV and put *BBC Breakfast* on to see if they'd announced William's name yet. It was Monday after all, and all of William's next of kin must have known about it by now.

He was back in the kitchen buttering his toast when he heard the local news start. He went into the living room with a butter-covered knife in hand and saw a picture of William Knight on screen.

It was a good picture of him. It must have been recent. He was smiling at the camera but not down its lens – whoever had taken the picture must've been close to him. Henry didn't think it was his mother.

There weren't many details about the case, just that the police had identified the body of the twenty-one-year-old man found stabbed near Addingham. They gave his name and said police inquiries were ongoing. Then they moved onto the next news item, which was about a school in Bradford trialing healthier school meals.

Henry switched off the TV and went back into the kitchen to finish buttering his toast. He wondered what this now meant for his investigation. He wouldn't be able to shock people with the news of William's death any longer, and he'd have to be especially careful when talking to people, so that they didn't think he was still in the police.

He couldn't risk another episode such as the one he'd had with Ben.

No, he thought, now was the time for snooping and looking into people from a distance. And if he really needed it, there was maybe a friend he could call who might give him some titbits of information – if his friend was still in the police.

* * *

Henry had showered, changed, and was sat at his computer in the spare room. There was a spare bed in the room, which he had for guests, but no one had ever slept in it apart from Tessa.

The room had a narrow window that looked out into Main Street. A double-decker bus went past slowly, and the commuters on the top deck could look right through the window and into the spare room if they chose to.

Henry wiped a layer of dust off the keyboard and blew on it. He had a five-year-old Apple iMac, which he'd bought when his last computer died suddenly. Someone had told him Apple computers didn't get viruses, so he went out and bought one. He still didn't know if they got viruses or not.

Its black screen was covered in dust, and he searched his desk and found an old microfibre cloth he used for his glasses folded up next to the white mouse. He wiped the screen until he could see his reflection and turned on the computer.

It took a few moments to boot up, then he went to the internet browser and searched for 'Companies House'. When its website came up, he straightened the notepad and pen on the desk next to him, and wondered what to search first. He didn't have Freddie's surname, so looking at every company director in the country whose first name was Freddie wouldn't be much use to him. Instead, he searched for 'Thistle Lodge'.

Some results came up. There was a firm that sold hot tubs, a care home in Lancashire, and some other business that was into selling cabins.

He scrolled down the results looking at addresses and eventually found what he was looking for: West Addingham Masonry.

Its address was Thistle Lodge, Addingham.

He felt a stir of excitement. This building enterprise had been established eleven years ago by two company directors; one of which was Frederic Burton. Its financial records were up to date, and, looking at the last tax return, Henry noted it made over a million a year. It seemed to do renovations and roof work, rather than building new properties.

Looking deeper into its financial records, he saw that West Addingham Masonry's finances had taken a hit during the pandemic, but Frederic Burton had loaned it enough cash to weather the storm.

Henry didn't need to think hard about where Freddie had found the money from.

Henry did another search on Companies House, this time using Freddie Burton's name. The search came up with several businesses that were all in the area. There was another building firm that no longer seemed to be active; two shops in Leeds city centre, one seemed to be an e-cigarette shop while the other sold art; then there was a bar in Ilkley, The Platform Edge.

Henry clicked on the bar's details and found that Frederic Burton had become its owner during the pandemic.

Henry sat back in his desk chair – an old wooden thing that gave his back problems if he sat in it for too long – and remembered his conversation with the manager at The Platform Edge. That fat, balding man. He wondered if he was Freddie, but then recalled that Ryan said Freddie was tall and blonde.

Anyway, he now had another link between Freddie and William. Freddie was his boss. He wondered what this meant as another double-decker bus rolled past his window, this time going in the opposite direction.

He leant forward and picked up his mobile phone, which was next to his notepad on his desk, and made a call to someone he thought could shine some light on all of this.

Chapter Twenty

Henry wasn't sure if the mobile number was still active but tried it anyway. He looked at the iMac's screen and caught the outline of his reflection in it. The phone call was placed, and it started ringing.

He picked up the pen and pulled the notepad across the desk so it was in reach. His pen was ready to jot down anything he needed.

He felt the ringing was nearing its end and that he would be put to voicemail, when his call was answered. "Is this really you?" The voice was loud, rich, and broad Yorkshire.

Henry couldn't help smiling upon hearing it. "Yes, it's me."

"Bloody hell. You're not dead then?"

Henry shook his head and felt his cheeks heat up. "No, nothing like that."

"I thought as much. I would've heard about it if you'd popped your clogs." He took a deep breath and then asked, "How long has it been? Must be three years?"

"Yes, it was Ashford's funeral," Henry said. Ashford had been their senior officer back in the day. He was his late eighties when he died of bowel cancer. Luckily it had happened before COVID, as Henry didn't think the old man would've coped well with being locked inside his house for months on end.

"Aye, it was. How you doing then, Ward?"

"Not bad. Keeping myself busy. How are things at West Yorkshire Police?"

He heard his old colleague take another long breath. "Complicated. I think I'm on my way out. It's getting scratchier and scratchier around here. You got out at the best possible time."

"Hmm," Henry said, doubtfully. "I have a different opinion about that."

"Yes. But you left before all the cuts and that nonsense. Anyway, I'm sure you're not calling me after all these years to hear me moan about my lot."

"Well, not really. I'm calling about a murder."

"Bloody hell, don't ask me for any details. You know what it's like. The higher up you get, the less you know what's going on in the streets. You don't think things are that bad until someone tries to mug you in your supermarket car park."

"Someone really tried to mug you?"

"He failed."

Henry didn't want to think about Detective Chief Inspector Murphy, in his late fifties and with an upper body as round as a barrel, tackling a potential supermarket mugger. "Anyway, I found a body in Addingham the other day."

"Addingham? A body?" He laughed down the phone. "Well, I'll never. And you found it?"

"Yes, I did. I thought I'd look into it, just to keep my mind sharp."

"Well, as long as you keep out of the way of our lot, I don't see any harm."

Henry remembered his conversation with DI Barnes then asked, "Have you heard of a DI Barnes?"

There were a few moments' silence down the line, then DCI Murphy said, "Nope. Must be new."

"She might be based in Wakefield. She's from down south, anyway, and has been on at me twice. Threatening me."

"Threatening? You? She must be new, then. Otherwise, she'd remember the days when you used to be a force to be reckoned with."

"Aye, well, those days are nearly gone. Sadly." He looked over at Tessa who had come into the spare room and was now preparing to jump onto the bed.

"Surely not. If she gives you any more grief, tell her DCI Murphy will be having words."

Henry felt slightly cheered up by that but went on to say, "Don't worry, I think I can manage her. Her bark's worse than her bite and all that."

DCI Murphy laughed. "Well, if you think so. Was there anything else? Only I'm supposed to be in a meeting shortly. Not that I don't dislike our chats, we should have more of them."

"Yes," Henry said, positioning his pen over the notepad again. "Have you heard of a drug dealer around my end called Freddie?"

DCI Murphy took a breath then said, "Freddie. I think it rings a bell, yes. Where's he based? Addingham?"

"Yes. He's from Leeds and owns a few businesses in the area."

"Hmm, and you think he's involved in this murder?"

"The lad that died had been to one of his drug-fuelled house parties."

"Ah, well, you've got him banged to rights then." He chuckled down the phone, then Henry heard him move some sheets of paper about. "You got a full name for him?"

"Frederic Burton, Leeds, now lives at Thistle Lodge in Addingham."

He heard DCI Murphy mumble the details to himself as he jotted them down. "I'll get an underling to look into it and pass whatever they get onto you. Everything, I'm sure, will be handled in the strictest of confidences," he said, though Henry almost heard him smiling as he said it.

"Of course."

"Very good. Well, Ward, it's been a pleasure talking to you after all these years."

"Aye, DCI Murphy, it really has."

* * *

Henry ended the call and stood up out of his chair. His armpits and back were hot underneath his navy woollen jumper. Excitement and adrenaline were rushing through his system.

He'd avoided calling for help until now, but he thought he needed it. Things were getting to that point. He also believed DCI Murphy when he said he'd deal with DI Barnes if she came at him again. Murphy had never been a fan of upstarts and had always been loyal to Henry, even after his fall from grace.

They'd been partners back in the day and worked together on numerous cases. Sitting in the same car during uncountable stakeouts and helping each other in a few fights. Then Murphy went off up the ladder, and so did Henry. Their paths didn't cross until Henry was in his last days, fending off the accusations against him and dealing with the inquiries. It was Murphy who replaced him after the higher-ups demanded that Henry retire early.

Henry had always wondered if Murphy had a part to play in his demise but didn't think so. He doubted his old partner was that untrustworthy, and there wasn't an ambition angle for him, as Murphy was already a DCI somewhere else. But still, the thought still lingered within him.

He waved his arms around the spare room to expel some of his pent-up energy, which unsettled the dusty air and woke up Tessa. He then went downstairs to his kitchen table.

Picking up his marker pen, he scribbled some notes on the edge of the page near Freddie's name, then wondered what he could do next while he waited on intel about him. He already knew he owned The Platform Edge and lived at Thistle Lodge so he could go watch either of them to see what he could learn, but he felt that would be a waste of time.

He turned over the crumpled sheet of A3 paper – some of the ink had bled through in places – and sat down on a chair at the table and started writing out a timeline for Friday night.

William had worked at The Platform Edge and left at 3 a.m., presumably with Louise, whom Henry made a note to talk to later.

They drove to Addingham, which was a ten-minute drive, and picked up Ryan Miller. Then they went to the party at Thistle Lodge, probably arriving around 3.30.

He marked these times on the top of the piece of paper then moved to the bottom. William was found by him at around 9.45 a.m., and Ryan said he left the party just before, at around 9 a.m.

He sat back in his chair and looked up at the white wall of his kitchen, though he wasn't looking at it, but trying to work out how long it would take to walk downhill from Thistle Lodge to the field where he'd found William.

Could Ryan have walked down the hill with William, then gone back up to the party before he got his taxi? Or had someone else walked with William?

He shook his head, feeling like he was forgetting something, and flipped over the A3 piece of paper. He scanned his notes, trying to distinguish his handwriting, when he saw two words: 'shoe' and 'sheep'. William's shoe was missing, and there was also a dead sheep, wasn't there? Could that have been involved somehow?

He got up from the kitchen table and stepped into the living room, where he saw Tessa's lead curled up on top of the dresser. He grabbed it then called up the staircase. "Wake up, lazybones. We're off for a walk!"

Chapter Twenty-One

It was windy on the hill above Addingham. The already windswept trees were blown further into submission by a strong breeze. Grey clouds growled in the sky, threatening another mixed day of rain followed by sunshine.

Henry got out of his Skoda Octavia, which he'd parked in the same spot as he'd done the previous day, and let out Tessa, who'd been barking the whole drive up. He put the lead on before she ran off then locked his car.

He had his anorak on, as the grey clouds looked bruised and angry. He looked about the lane, where his car was squeezed up against a drystone wall, and tried to find a public footpath. There wasn't one. Instead, he called Tessa to heel and they walked up the lane towards Thistle Lodge.

He passed the farm where he'd seen the Border collie the previous day. The dog was no longer there. He suspected she was out working in the fields, herding sheep or whatever it was she did.

He paused for a moment. Sheep. He walked towards the livestock gate and looked into the muck-covered farmyard. Tessa seemed to be getting excited by the smell of other animals. Her little tail wagged back and forth.

There was no one in the farmyard, so he decided he'd talk to the farmer on his way back up the hill. If he wasn't too tired.

He continued up the lane and walked past the empty modernist house. He peered through its large windows and looked in its empty rooms. He didn't like the feeling those empty rooms gave him and carried on. He made a mental note to ask Mrs Whitehead what she'd found out about the place. He didn't think it was related to William's murder somehow, but he had a feeling that there was something odd about it.

He walked past Thistle Lodge. There wasn't any dance music to be heard now. He peered over the old wooden fence, which was green with moss in places, and looked into the gravel-filled courtyard. The modern silver Land Rover wasn't there. He was tempted to open the gate and walk in and have a look around but decided not to risk it.

Instead, he continued up the lane, past the house, with Tessa by his side. The houses became sparser the further he went, and he knew eventually there'd be nothing but rolling hills, heather, bogs and the occasional grouse until the Cow and Calf Rocks in Ilkley.

Eventually, he saw a crooked wooden fence in the drystone wall and walked through it. It was on a spring-loaded hinge, and it slapped back into place, hitting a well-beaten post. He was in a field that gently rolled down the hill towards Addingham in the valley below.

He took out his phone and opened the stopwatch application he'd found earlier. He started it and followed Tessa down the hill. He wouldn't be as fast as Ryan would've been, but at least this experiment would give him a vague idea of how long it might take to walk down and up that hill.

He let Tessa off the lead, and she went running off, stretching her legs as she went. He followed her with his gaze then looked down at the tuffs of wild grass in the field. Had William walked down here? He looked about the grass in case he found anything. But after a few days' rain, he doubted he'd find anything that would have any DNA left on it.

He heard barking and looked down the field. At the bottom of the gentle slope was another gate in the drystone wall. Tessa stood there, barking at something.

He shook his head and hoped it was a grouse hiding in a tall tuft of grass. If she'd found that shoe, he wouldn't know how to explain himself to DI Barnes.

He trudged down the gentle incline, watching his footing so he didn't trip up, and eventually joined Tessa at the gate. She was sniffing around its gatepost and barking. Not an angry bark. It was one she used when she wanted attention for something.

He stooped over and looked at the gatepost and peered at the tall grass around it. He couldn't see anything and felt some relief that it was a false alarm.

Tessa kept on barking, and he hushed her then knelt down to put her lead back on, but she wasn't having any of it. She got up on her back legs and scratched at the gatepost.

He wondered what she wanted and pushed the gate open. Immediately she ran through the gap and to the gatepost on the other side.

Feeling a sense of unease, he followed her through the gate and saw something sparkle in the grass. "What on the earth?"

He knelt down and budged Tessa out of the way. Taking out a handkerchief from his anorak pocket, he covered his fingers with it and pulled out a mobile phone from the grass.

Should he call it in? He didn't know what to do. He placed William's mobile phone back in the grass as if he hadn't touched it and looked around. There didn't seem to be any other evidence. Looking back at the phone, he almost managed to persuade himself that it could be someone else's. Maybe some hiker who'd had trouble with the gate and hadn't realised that his phone had dropped out of his pocket.

But no. He was pretty sure it was William's phone he was looking at. He pulled out his own mobile phone from his pocket and paused the stopwatch, which showed ten minutes had passed since he'd set off.

Who should he call? Would DCI Murphy be of any use to him? Or should he call the general police number? He didn't have DI Barnes's number. Besides, he didn't want to speak with her.

He settled on the general police number and called the operator. After a difficult conversation, where the woman on the other end of the line couldn't see the emergency in an old man finding a phone in a field, he lost his nerve and asked to be put through to someone on the investigation for William Knight's murder.

He was transferred to three different numbers before he spoke to someone on the murder investigation. Probably a young, over-worked DC.

"Hello," Henry said. "I'm calling about the murder of William Knight. I think I've just found his phone."

This pricked the interest of the DC. "Can you repeat that?"

"Yes, I've just found the phone of William Knight. I think. It's in a field not too far from where he was found." Henry looked further down the incline and saw, a few fields away, the one where he'd found William.

"Right. And you are?"

Henry cleared his throat and put on his most authoritative voice. "Henry Ward."

Henry could almost hear the penny drop on the other end of the line. "Former DCI Henry Ward?"

Henry didn't know what the DC's tone meant and said, "That's me."

"Ah, DI Barnes has mentioned your name."

"I bet she has." He looked down at the phone. "Do you want this phone or not? It's been in the rain for two days, but I'm sure one of your techies can find something on it."

"Yes," the DC said. "I'll come on out and get it. Can you wait for me? I wouldn't know which field it was in."

Henry sighed and looked up at the grey clouds that were rolling over the valley. "How long will you be?"

"Twenty minutes."

"I suppose you wouldn't want me to pick up the phone so I can sit in my car with it?"

"Don't touch it." He heard the DC move around on the other end. "I'll be there as soon as I can."

Chapter Twenty-Two

Henry took the chance, while it wasn't raining, to walk further down the hill to the field where he'd found William. He restarted the stopwatch so he could time it.

Tessa was off her lead and ran into the field like she was back in a play area where she'd found lots of different goodies. She ran to the spot where the dead sheep had once lain and sniffed the grass. Apart from the clumps of wool that clung to some of the shards of grass, there was no sign that a dead sheep had been there.

Tessa got bored then ran off into the next field where they'd found William. Henry followed behind, not out of breath, but feeling his lungs struggle. He should've taken another dose of his inhaler before he'd set off.

He stood at the spot where the sheep had been and looked up at the way he'd come. Was the sheep connected to this somehow? He had no idea how it could be. He looked over at the field in which they'd found William and followed Tessa into it.

Tessa was sniffing the drystone wall. There wasn't any police tape or anything. The scene of crime officers must have done their best, but there's not much they could do with a body in a soggy field.

He walked up the hill to the drystone wall then turned his back on it and looked around. William had come to lie here. He'd walked down from Thistle Lodge and ended up here. Henry took out his phone and looked at the stopwatch. It said twenty-five minutes. Now, assuming Ryan was faster than sixty-three-year-old Henry with his asthma and bad hip, he'd probably make that in less than twenty minutes.

What if Ryan had walked down the hill with William, then something happened, and Ryan ran back up the hill and returned to the party. It'd take him around forty minutes to walk down and back up, counting twenty minutes each way. If Ryan got his taxi at 9 a.m., William must've been stabbed around 8 a.m.

Henry shook his head. He didn't think Ryan was the killer, but he thought he was hiding something. His excuse of being too high at the party to remember anything was a bit weak.

He looked around the spot again then turned to the drystone wall and patted a rough slab of limestone. "We'll get to the bottom of this, William."

He called Tessa to heel, put her lead back on, and started his climb back up the hill.

* * *

Henry made it back to the gate where he'd found William's phone. He was wheezing, and Tessa looked bored as she'd been on the lead and had to go at his pace. His left hip was burning again, and he felt like he needed a sit down and a cup of tea.

Luckily the grey clouds that sat over the valley hadn't opened yet. He peered down the tall grass around the gatepost and saw William's phone was still there. Daylight reflected off its black screen.

He heard some grouse squawking in a nearby field, and Tessa growled. She liked chasing them, though Henry didn't let her do it, as he felt for the grouse who weren't as quick as a sprinting dog.

A silver car pulled up at the drystone wall near the top of the hill. After a few moments, a short man wearing a dark-grey overcoat walked through the gate then down the field.

Henry watched him approach. He was slightly overweight and seemed to be watching where he was putting his dress shoes. He called out to Henry when he was twenty feet away. "DCI Ward?"

Henry nodded. "I'm retired. So, you can call me Mr Ward."

The man pulled out an ID card from the inside pocket of his overcoat and said, "DC Nichols."

"Nice to meet you," Henry said, sizing up this Nichols. "It's down here, the phone."

Henry held the gate open for Nichols and then pointed down into the thick grass. "The dog found it."

"Clever dog," Nichols said, looking at Tessa. She looked up at him and wagged her tale.

Nichols put on plastic gloves then took out his own mobile phone, which seemed to be huge, and started taking pictures of the area around the gate. Henry imagined they'd be printed off and stuck on a board in an investigation room, that was if they still did that. Maybe it was all online these days.

After a few minutes, Nichols seemed satisfied with the photos and took out a see-through plastic evidence bag. He bent down, picked up the phone, then put it in the bag. "Have you seen anything else around here that might be related to the investigation?"

Henry shook his head.

Nichols stood up and put the phone in his pocket. "You were the one that found him?"

Henry nodded, wondering where he was going with this.

"Is it far from here, the place where you found him?"

Henry shook his head and pointed down the moorside to the field. "It's over there."

"Want to join me as I go take a look?"

Henry thought it was an odd question, and almost declined the offer, as his lungs and hips were both burning. Instead, he said, "All right. It's a ten-minute walk."

Nichols nodded. He had short dark hair, dark eyes, and a dark beard. Everyone seemed to have beards these days, and Henry didn't know why. There was a sweet, oaky smell coming off him, which Henry guessed was his aftershave. "So, it must be odd for you to stumble back into a case after all these years," Nichols said.

Henry grunted a non-committal reply. He didn't know where Nichols was going yet.

"My dad," Nichols said, looking off into the field, "he didn't cope well with retirement. He might've done with a few cases like this."

Henry gave the young detective a sideways glance. "What did he do? Was he police?"

"No, he was in the fire service. He was retired out due to ill health. He'd have liked to have kept himself busy."

"Right," Henry said. He looked at Nichols and saw nothing but sincerity. If he was aiming an attack at him, he was going about it in an odd way. "Is he still around, your dad?"

Nichols shook his head then pointed to the field. "Is that it?"

"Yes, that's the one."

They both walked through the gate and across the grass.

"It's just up here," Henry said.

Tessa pulled at her lead as they crossed the point where the sheep had been.

"Here's something odd," Henry said, "I found a dead sheep at this spot."

Nichols stopped and looked at the grass. "Here?"

Henry nodded. "I found it the same morning I found William's body. I don't know if it's related, but…"

Nichols took out his huge phone again and took more pictures of the grass. When he was done, he turned to Henry and asked, "Who owns this land?"

"I think that farmer on the top of the hill keeps his sheep here."

Nichols put his huge phone in his pocket and nodded. "I'll have a chat with him later."

They walked through the field then back to the spot where Henry had found William. "It was here."

Nichols climbed up the hill towards the drystone wall and took more pictures with his phone. "Did you see anyone around when you found him?"

Henry shook his head. "Just me and the dog."

Nichols finished taking pictures and looked around the field. He pointed towards Addingham in the distance. "He was walking back home?"

Henry didn't say anything, he just watched.

"That means" – Nichols looked over towards the top of the moorside – "he'd been up there."

Henry could bite his lip no longer. "How far have you lot got in this investigation?"

Nichols smiled. "Not that far, unfortunately. But it's funny, really, as I was going to ask you the same thing."

Chapter Twenty-Three

The heavens had opened, and the rain pelted Nichols' car's windscreen. Tessa was sat on his back seat, on top of an old fleece. The vehicle smelled of mints and had that stuffy new-car smell.

They'd made it back just after the rain had started, and Henry's jeans were damp. He'd left his anorak on, though he'd brushed off some of the water before he sat down on the new leather seats.

"So, let's hear what you've got, Mr Ward." Nichols was leaning forward on the steering wheel, chewing gum.

Henry shook his head. "Let's hear what you've got first."

Nichols leant back into his leather seat and stared out the windscreen at the rain. "Not much, to be fair. As you've probably realised, there's no CCTV around here, and no witnesses. We're not even sure where he'd been."

Henry felt some accomplishment that he'd got further than the police.

Nichols pulled out William's phone from his overcoat pocket. It was still in its plastic bag. "Hopefully, we'll be able to get some data from here."

"If it isn't too water-damaged."

Nichols looked at the phone and nodded. "Most phones are fairly waterproof these days."

"Any chance you'll let me know what's on it?" Henry asked.

Nichols shook his head. "Not until you tell me what you've found out."

Henry looked out the windscreen and at the rain. It pelted the roof and ran down the sides of the car. "I was under the impression that DI Barnes didn't want me involved."

"She doesn't. But that doesn't mean I don't want to know what you've found out."

Henry kept his lips shut tight and folded his arms. The sleeves of his anorak were still damp.

"Listen, I don't mind you getting involved. I know who you were. DI Barnes doesn't. She just thinks you're an old fogey who was kicked out of the police because of corruption."

"I wasn't kicked out," Henry said.

"I know." He held up his hands in defence. "But she doesn't know that. She just doesn't want you messing up her case when it goes to trial."

"I won't mess anything up, I'm not an idiot."

"I know. You're DCI Ward." He looked out the window. "I've heard about you. I heard you didn't take any prisoners and that."

"I didn't."

He then looked back at Henry. "I also heard you're still connected with the people upstairs."

Henry nodded. "A few. The ones that are still there." Then he realised what this was. DI Barnes didn't want him to be involved in the investigation in case he caused problems for her, while DC Nichols wanted to humour Henry so he would put a good word in for him with the current higher-ups. "What is this, DC Nichols? Think you can become a detective sergeant by humouring me?"

Nichols smiled and laughed to himself. "No. I think solving a few cases and having you as someone I can rely on will help me to become a DS."

"You want me as someone you can rely on?"

He nodded. "It doesn't hurt to know a few people higher up the food chain."

"I'm no longer on the food chain if you haven't noticed."

"Aye, but you know people who are still on it."

Henry leant his head against the back of the leather headrest. "So, you want me to tell you what I know so you can go solve this case and get the glory?"

Nichols shook his head. "No, because I'd like to have friends who stick around. You wouldn't stick around if I did that."

"So?"

"Like I said before, tell me what you know, and I'll tell you what's on this phone." The plastic bag crackled as he lifted up the phone.

"When you find out what's on it?"

Nichols nodded.

"What if I tell you everything and you don't tell me what's on the phone?"

"Well, you know some of my senior officers, so I wouldn't risk that."

Henry looked at the young detective. He was very sure of himself, and there was a hunger behind his eyes, a hunger to better himself and get ahead. Henry had a faint memory of what that felt like. "Alright, in exchange for what I know, I want to know what's on that phone and to have updates on your investigation."

Nichols clenched his jaw to show he thought Henry was driving a hard bargain. "Deal." He held out a well-moisturised hand for Henry to shake.

* * *

The rain had finished, and water dripped off the branches of the windswept trees and straggly bushes that lined the side of the road. Tessa snored peacefully in the back of Nichols' car. They'd been in there so long the windows had steamed up, and Henry's backside was numb from sitting down.

"So, you think this Freddie had a party, that William left it, walking down the hill, then something happened to him there?" Nichols had his huge phone out and was typing notes into it.

Henry nodded. He'd eventually given up and accepted Nichols' offer of some chewing gum, which tasted too strongly of mint for him. The air in the car was getting stuffy, and he wanted to open the window. Nichols' aftershave was also getting to him, tickling the back of his throat so he felt like he could lapse into a coughing fit at any moment.

"Do you think it's this Ryan Miller?" Nichols asked.

"I don't think it's him. Only that he's involved somehow."

"There's also this Louise. Do you have a surname for her?"

He shook his head. "She works at The Platform Edge."

"Which is owned by Freddie?"

Henry nodded. He'd seen lots of detectives in his time and knew how to rank them based on their skills. He'd seen some exceptional ones who could pick up an obscure detail and connect it to the case. He'd also seen those that had to bargain and bully their way through investigations. They rarely hung around for long, especially these days. He ranked himself as being nearer the top end, based on the number of cases he'd closed and how quickly he rose up the ranks. He rated DC Nichols as being a little above average. The young detective still had a lot to learn, but there was potential within him.

"So, what does this all show you?" Henry asked in a teacherly voice.

Nichols frowned, aware that he was being tested and not liking it. He played along anyway. "Well, something happened at the party, which caused William to walk down the hill to the spot where he died."

"Okay, that's the basics. Was he stabbed at the party or after?"

Nichols covered his mouth with his hand as he considered his answer. "After. They'd have been fewer witnesses. Probably in the field."

Henry agreed. He didn't know how many people had been at the party, but he suspected one of them would've talked if they'd have seen William getting stabbed. "So, who stabbed him and why?"

"Love triangle," Nichols said. "That Louise and Ryan."

Henry had considered the same thing but wasn't sure if it was a goer. "Possibly. Or it was something to do with drugs."

"What makes you think that?"

Henry frowned and looked at him. "What do you know about the case?"

He shrugged. "I know about as much as you."

"Don't you know about the drugs in William's pocket?"

"Drugs? What drugs?"

Henry felt his cheeks redden, because, by mentioning the drugs, he'd admitted to a police detective that he'd unlawfully searched William's pockets. "There were drugs in William's pocket."

"Were there?" Nichols looked completely confused then pored over his notes on the phone.

"Yes, there was a big bag of something on him."

Nichols looked through his notes then said, "I can't find anything about drugs."

Henry felt a metallic taste in the back of his throat. What was going on? He'd seen the drugs in William's pocket, hadn't he?

Nichols leant back in his chair. "Wait a minute? You looked through William's pockets when you found him?"

Henry met his glance and nodded. "Well, the dog found the drugs, I just stopped her from pulling the bag out of his pocket and eating it all."

Nichols nodded like he was willing to accept Henry's story then he pulled a face. "Where did the drugs go then? If there were any."

Henry stared through the windscreen at the fields outside. "There definitely were some. I don't have the habit of imagining bags of drugs on corpses."

Nichols was silent a moment then said, "Well, if you found the drugs and they've not been put in the report…"

"Then someone took the drugs off him before he got to the hospital or someone didn't write it into the report," Henry said, finishing his thought.

Nichols stared off into the distance as well. "Who'd do that?"

"I don't know." Henry waited a moment before asking, "Do you trust your colleagues?"

Nichols straightened up. "I don't like what you're implying."

"Well, let's look into both options. Either one of the uniformed officers swiped the bag from William's pocket, or one of the ambulance crew. Or someone in your office didn't write them up and destroyed the evidence."

"Hang on!" Nichols put his hand up as if to say 'stop'. "You're not considering the most likely explanation: that there's been a cock-up. The drugs either fell out of his pocket while he was being wheeled to the ambulance, or they were found but no one bothered to type it up."

"Have things gotten that bad now in the police?" Henry said, shaking his head.

"Oi, like everything was above board and proper in your time."

Henry felt the barb and relented. "Alright, what do you propose to do, then? I've looked at the spot where we found William twice today and nothing was there."

"Aye, but did you look around the spot where the ambulance wheeled him away on the stretcher?"

Henry sighed as he knew where this was going. His backside was completely numb, apart from his left hip which growled with an intense burn. "No, and I can't be bothered going to have a look." He gave Nichols his home address and turned to wake up Tessa. "Call in for a cup of tea once you've had a look."

"Why? Where are you going?"

"Back home. I'll leave the searching of bushes for bags of drugs to you. I am retired after all."

Chapter Twenty-Four

Henry opened his front door to let Tessa inside. The sun was out now, shining on all the plants in his front yard. His eyes had become accustomed to an overcast sky, so he had to squint to look at them.

The lavender smelt sweet and strong, and he leant over the chimney pot to smell them. A fuzzy, round bumblebee leapt off the purple flowers and flew into the air, nearly causing Henry to jump back.

He was halfway in the house when a double-decker bus drove past his gate at the same time as Mrs Whitehead called out his name. Her call was obscured by the bus's engine, so she called again. "Henry!"

He turned and looked at her. "Yes?"

She was wearing a white blazer over a multi-coloured blouse and white jeans and stood on her doorstep, waving for him to come over. He rolled his eyes then told Tessa to behave as he closed the front door on her and locked it.

Inside Mrs Whitehead's, she told him to take a seat on her sofa. He tried to brush away her dark grey cat, which was sat on it, but it just scowled at him. "Do you want tea?" she asked him.

Henry shook his head and perched on the edge of the sofa, keeping his distance from her cat. The burn in his left hip was taking up most of his attention. He needed some painkillers soon or he'd start snapping at people. He didn't want to snap at Mrs Whitehead as he didn't know what she'd do to him if he did.

She sat down in her chair next to the knitting box and turned off the TV with the remote. "Two things. Mrs Miller asked if you could call in later?"

He raised an eyebrow.

"She says young Ryan's beginning to remember more things about the party. Says she wants you to chat to him in case the police call by."

"Aye, alright." He wondered what it was that young Ryan had remembered, or more accurately, what it was that he was prepared to talk about. "And the second thing. I found out who owned the modernist house."

He remembered that modern-looking house on the hill near Thistle Lodge. He leant forward. "Who is it then?"

"Well, it's some old family that originally came from Ilkley. Apparently, they had it built back in the 1950s, and no one's lived there for nearly twenty years."

"Do you know the name of the family?"

"The Mortons."

He hadn't heard of the name. "And the house has been empty for twenty years?"

She nodded. "Apparently there's a gardener who goes up and sees to the land, and there's a cleaner who goes in once a month to make sure it's still standing. But yeah. It's been left like that for twenty years."

"That's a bit odd, isn't it? Why not just sell it?"

"Well, that's what I asked. I was speaking to Bryan Harrison, you know, he's on the parish council and has lived here his whole life. He's got that big house down by the river. He says a young couple of the family moved into the house just after they were married, but then something happened, and they moved away. The whole family."

"The whole family? How many of them were they?"

She shook his head. "He didn't know for sure. But something funny happened in that house."

He thought about its wide windows and white walls and the old carpets that no one walked on. "Odd. It does give me a funny feeling that house, like something went on there."

"Well, now you know something did. We just don't know what."

"Hmm." He nodded and wondered if he'd ever find out. "Who owns the farm next to it?"

She narrowed her eyes as she tried to think of the answer then nodded her head. "Oh, you mean the sheep farm next door? I think it's a family called the Taylors. They've been there for years. He breeds sheepdogs, I think. They're award winners and were in the paper. Why?"

"I think one of his sheep's involved with William's death."

She pulled a face. "You think a sheep killed him?"

"No. I think someone killed a sheep."

"Why would they do that?" As she asked the question, she spun her head around and looked through her window. "A silver car's just pulled up outside yours. Some young guy's driving it."

Henry stood up and winced as he put weight on his left hip. "That'll be the police for me."

"The police? What happened to that blonde detective?"

"Her colleague's actually interested in hearing what I've got to say."

She rolled her eyes then went back to looking out of her window. "That makes a change."

* * *

Henry had to squeeze past Nichols' silver Ford Focus to open his front gate. He'd parked it on the pavement to let the traffic flow up and down Main Street. Nichols got out of the car, still wearing his dark grey overcoat, and nodded at Henry.

"Did you find it?" Henry asked, remembering the bag of drugs he'd sent Henry out to look for.

Nichols grinned and blew a bubble with his chewing gum.

Henry let him inside his house and offered him tea, which Nichols accepted. Before he went into the kitchen, he hobbled over to the dresser in the living room and opened up the drawer where he kept his painkillers. He grabbed the packet and told Nichols to take a seat.

Henry then went into the kitchen and put the kettle on before swallowing two pills with a glass of water.

He glanced at his notes on the kitchen table and turned over the A3 sheet of paper and scribbled some notes down on the back of it. He heard Nichols come into his kitchen, his dress shoes clacking on the tiles. "What's this?"

Henry felt slightly exposed and looked at him. "What do you think?"

Nichols leant over the kitchen table and read the notes. "You've done quite a bit on this. I thought you hadn't done that much?"

"I never said that," Henry said, going to the kettle to pour water into two empty cups. "It's kept me busy." He let Nichols read his notes then asked, "So, you found the bag of drugs?"

Nichols nodded and pulled out another evidence bag from his overcoat pocket, which he was still wearing. The packet of drugs was held inside the evidence bag. It was a yellowy white powder that could pass for sherbet.

"Where was it?"

"In some nettles along the footpath that leads into the village." He looked at the bag in his hand. "It must've fallen out while they were moving his body along the footpath."

Henry shook his head in disbelief. He'd never heard anything like that happening before. "How could the uniforms have missed that? Not to mention the ambulance crew? Didn't they put him in a bag before they rolled his stretcher down that footpath?"

Nichols shrugged. "People are overworked. They stopped caring about dropping small details like that years ago. Now it's endemic."

Henry shook his head at the mess things were in then took out the two teabags and handed one of the cups to Nichols, who nodded his thanks as he took it. Nichols then spat his chewing gum out into a tissue he'd had in his pocket.

Henry pulled out one of the chairs from under the kitchen table, its legs squeaking against the tiles, and sat down. Nichols followed his lead and pulled out the second one.

"So," Henry said, sipping his tea, "we've got the drug angle, which I think has stronger legs than the love triangle one. Young Ryan Miller wants to speak with me again later on today."

"You've already spoken to him?"

Henry nodded. "Yesterday. I said I could help him prepare his story for the police."

Nichols dark eyes went serious. "I hope you weren't coaching him to not tell us the truth when we eventually got round to talking to him."

"I wasn't. I was just preparing him by asking him the kind of questions I would have asked if I wasn't retired."

Nichols seemed alright with that and asked, "What did he say?"

"Not much. He couldn't remember what had happened at the party. But now, apparently, he can."

"We can go pay him a visit?"

Henry frowned as he looked at him. "Don't you have stuff to be getting on with?"

Nichols sipped his tea then said, "Looks like I'm getting more done hanging around you."

Henry shook his head as he thought about the old days. "I used to train detectives, you know? I did it for a few years before they moved me up the ladder."

"I know. Why d'you think I'm here?"

Chapter Twenty-Five

He let Nichols out of his house then locked the door. The sun was quite strong now, and the wood panelling on his front door was hot. He'd like to sit in his front yard and read a book but knew he couldn't. He had to go question young Ryan Miller.

Nichols' car was causing some grief on the narrow Main Street and Nichols checked the side exposed to the traffic for any scratches. Satisfied, he then asked Henry where the Millers lived.

"Just behind the pub," Henry said.

Nichols nodded, and they crossed Main Street together when they saw a gap in the traffic. They walked past the tables outside the pub. Its patrons were enjoying the sun and their drinks. Nichols looked at the squat building covered in ivy and said, "I think I've heard of that pub. It looks quite nice."

"It's alright. Quite expensive." Henry looked towards the passageway as they walked through the pub's car park, which now had more cars in it than it'd had the night before. Then he remembered what had happened the previous night while he'd been walking in the opposite direction. "Oh, here's something that'd interest you."

"What?"

"I was assaulted in this car park last night?"

"By whom?"

"Young lad who worked with William at The Platform Edge. He's called Ben. I don't have his surname."

Nichols frowned. "You want me to look into it?"

Henry shook his head. "Don't. He only pushed me over. He'd gotten the wrong end of the stick about my employment status and your DI Barnes wound him up."

Nichols didn't seem convinced about dropping it. "Right, and he jumped out on you in this car park and knocked you over? At night?"

Henry nodded.

"Doesn't that make you think he'd be violent enough to stab William?"

Henry thought about it then shook his head. "We're all potentially violent enough to stab someone in the right circumstances."

The thought seemed to trouble Nichols as they walked down the alley, their footsteps echoing off its high concrete walls.

"Are you sure you want to come in and speak to the Millers' lad?" Henry asked. "I got the impression they wouldn't talk to the police without having a lawyer present."

"Really? Just for a chat?" He took a deep breath. "I can always make it official and take him down to the station."

"But then I wouldn't be able to be present, would I?"

Nichols shook his head. "You wouldn't. But that sounds like your problem."

"Well, I know what questions to ask him, and you don't. So that sounds more like your problem."

They reached the end of the alleyway and joined the pavement that ran alongside the road heading to Bolton Abbey. There was a beck gurgling nearby that could be heard when there was no traffic.

"How about we just play it cool?" Nichols said. "Make it seem like it's just a chat, and if things get serious, I'll make things official."

Henry nodded. The painkillers had kicked in, and he could no longer feel his left hip burn, but his mind was less sharp. He'd probably struggle to do any mental arithmetic. "All right, let's see what happens. But let me do the talking."

They arrived at the Millers' house, which Nichols commented was 'amazing', and Henry pressed the intercom button next to their reinforced gate. They were let in and walked towards the Roman-style porch, where Becky Miller was standing at the front door.

"Mr Ward?" she asked, sounding as if she was really asking who Nichols was. She'd almost completely closed the front door behind her.

Nichols pulled out his ID and presented himself to her. She looked at Henry, her eyes suggesting she felt betrayed, and asked, "Henry?"

"He's with me," Henry said, feeling his head spin slightly from the painkillers. "He's alright, he just wants to hear what Ryan has to say. I'll do the talking, he'll just observe."

She pulled a face like she wasn't having it. "I'd rather call in a lawyer first–"

"Mrs Miller," Nichols interrupted, "you're fully entitled to have a lawyer–"

"I know I am."

"But if you want to make this an official interview, then I'll place your son under caution, and he'll spend the rest of the day down at Bradford police station. He might even stay overnight; it depends when I get round to talking to him."

There was a look of horror on Becky Miller's face. The thought of her poor son in a lock-up in Bradford turned her skin a pale white.

"Or," Nichols continued, "we can talk to your son here and now."

She considered it. Her mouth was slightly agape like she was either about to snap at them or tell them to come in.

"Mrs Miller," Henry said. She looked at him. "We'll be half an hour. We have a few questions then we'll be gone. Otherwise, DC Nichols here will take him over to Bradford where he'll be processed."

"Alright," she said, opening the door wide enough for them to enter.

* * *

Ryan was sat at the kitchen island. He looked just as pale as the previous day, but his eyes were less bloodshot. Mr Miller didn't seem to be there, though there was the faint smell of espresso in the air, which Henry took as a sign that he was in.

Ryan looked up nervously from his hands which were clasped in front of him on the island's oak tabletop. His eyes widened as he saw Nichols.

"This is DC Nichols," Henry explained. "He's working on William's murder, and he wants to sit and watch while I ask you some questions. Do you understand?"

Ryan looked just about ready to jump off the stool he was sat on and run upstairs. But Becky Miller remained at the kitchen doorway, blocking his route. She had her arms folded in front of her chest and said, "Answer their questions, Ryan, otherwise they'll take you to Bradford."

Ryan's eyes widened. "Bradford?"

"Police station," said Nichols. "Where we'll keep you overnight until we get round to interviewing you formally."

Ryan stared down at the oak tabletop of the kitchen island. He went even paler. Henry sat down opposite him while Nichols remained standing nearby with his hands in the pockets of his overcoat.

"So, do you remember what happened at the party?" Henry asked.

Ryan shrugged.

"What can you tell us?"

Ryan looked up from the oak tabletop. "I was pretty high. I can't remember much."

"What were you taking?"

Ryan looked down at the tabletop again, and Henry became aware of Becky Miller's presence in the room, in the sight line of her son.

Henry turned to her and asked, "Mrs Miller? Would you mind leaving us a few minutes?"

Her face flushed with rage. "I do mind."

"It's just that, young Ryan here might not want his mum knowing what he gets up to at parties."

She looked ready to argue her case but shook her head instead. "Oh, I don't care. I've had enough of this."

She waved her hands in the air as if she was throwing the situation away and stormed off down the hallway. A door banged, and Henry assumed it belonged to the living room.

Henry exhaled. He looked up at Nichols who widened his eyes as if to say, 'She's intense'.

Henry leant forward, resting his elbows on the oak tabletop. "Right, Ryan, your mum's not here, and whatever you tell us won't be relayed back to her. So, what drugs were you taking at that party on Friday night?"

Ryan didn't move for a moment, he just stared at the tabletop, then he took in a breath and said, "Weed. Some MDMA. A lot of coke."

Henry felt some relief. The lad was finally talking. "Alright, where did you get them from?"

He sighed again before saying, "The weed was mine. I got that off a dealer in Ilkley. The rest had been from the party."

"Did someone at the party hand the stuff to you?"

Ryan smiled. "No, it was all on the table."

"On the table?"

"Yeah, like a small buffet. There's a huge bowl of skunk in the centre, then little bowls with MDMA, coke, ketamine, whatever you want."

Henry took a moment to imagine it. "And it's all there and free to use?"

Ryan nodded. "Take what you want. Just as long as you don't OD or anything. Freddie said if anyone OD'd, they'd be dragged into a field and left for dead."

Henry felt a slight chill run down his back. "He said that? That people would be dragged into a field?"

Ryan, having realised what he'd said, went on, "I think it was a joke."

"Did you ever see anyone OD and be dragged anywhere?"

He shook his head. "It was a joke. He was just messing around."

Henry looked at Nichols, who didn't give what he was thinking away, then back to Ryan. "And it was all free? Freddie didn't want anything in return?"

Ryan shrugged. "He never asked me. He just seemed to have people over and that was how he enjoyed himself."

"How many people were there on Friday night?"

Ryan blew air out of his lips then said, "Thirty."

"Thirty people? What did you all do, besides take drugs?"

"Danced. He's converted one of the old barns into a nightclub. There's a bar and one of his mates DJs. Then, there are like chill-out spots around the house. And a few bedrooms for people to go into if they want."

"Where did you spend your time at the party?"

He sniffed. "In the barn, dancing, then I went into some of the chill-out spots when I wanted to sit down."

"Were you with William or Louise?"

He shook his head. "I lost them earlier on in the night. They both went off together."

Henry leant backwards on the uncomfortable stool and tried to readjust his legs. He glanced at Nichols who was still standing nearby with his hands in his pockets.

"Do you know what William did at the party?" Henry asked.

Ryan shook his head. "He drank some beers. He'd already had a few at work, I think. Then he smoked some spliffs and danced with me and Louise, then they both went off somewhere."

"Do you know where?"

He shook his head. "Maybe to one of the bedrooms or one of the chill-out spots. But I didn't speak to him for the rest of the night."

"And who did you speak to?"

He shrugged again. "Everyone. We're all pretty sociable when we're high. Everyone's your new best friend."

"Do you know if William took any cocaine or any of the other drugs?"

Ryan shook his head.

"Had you seen him take drugs before?"

He nodded. "We'd shared lines before, but he said he was trying to get off it."

"Then why did he go to the party?"

Ryan looked down at the tabletop. "I don't know, apparently he didn't want to go, but it was Louise's idea."

"Louise's idea? How do you mean?"

"She wanted him to go with her. I think she was up to something."

Chapter Twenty-Six

"Louise was up to something?" Henry asked.

Nichols was now leaning against the far wall of the Millers' kitchen, his hands still in his overcoat pockets, watching Ryan speak. The espresso scent hung in the air, and Henry felt like he could do with a cup. The painkillers were at work and had slowed down his thinking. It was taking an extraordinary amount of effort to keep one step ahead of Ryan.

Ryan leant back on his stool. "She's always up to something."

"In what way?"

"She... I don't know... she's always conniving or planning something. And she normally managed to drag Will into it."

"Were they together?"

"Kind of. They slept together sometimes, but he liked guys as well."

Henry heard Nichols clear his throat and got the message. Was this the love triangle? Louise with William and William with Ryan?

"Were you involved?" Henry asked, feeling the need to clear his throat too after asking.

Ryan's pale cheeks went the lightest shade of red. "Involved?"

"With either William or Louise? You know?" Henry nodded his head so he wouldn't have to say 'sexually'.

Ryan looked down at his hands which rested on the tabletop. The fingers of each hand were clasped together. "Sometimes, with Will."

"You were 'involved' with him?"

Ryan met his stare and nodded. "We fooled around a few times… I think I liked him more than he liked me."

Henry glanced at Nichols who started to look a bit smug. He'd brought up the love triangle first, hadn't he? Henry had thought about it, but in a more outdated way. He still felt the drugs were important, though. "Were you jealous that he was with Louise?"

Ryan shook his head. "No. He wasn't really 'with' her. It was just when they were both messed up enough, they slept together."

"Was that what it was like between him and you?"

Ryan gave Henry that hostile frown he'd got from his mother as he considered Henry's question. Then his eyes widened as if he'd had a major realisation. "Probably. For him, maybe."

Henry glanced at Nichols again then looked down at his overcoat pocket, the one in which he was keeping the bag of drugs. Nichols met his gaze and seemed to understand what Henry was suggesting. He nodded, then pulled out the evidence bag and dumped it in the middle of the kitchen island's oak tabletop.

Ryan's eyes widened and he sat back on the stool. His eyes searched the large bag of drugs, which was the size of a tennis ball, tied shut with an elastic band.

"Have you seen this bag before?" Henry asked.

Ryan shook his head. "What is it?"

"Which drugs? I don't know, but DC Nichols here will find out and we'll be able to tell you then."

Ryan still stared at the bag of drugs on his mum's kitchen island.

"We found it on William's body. Would you know why he'd have a big bag like this on him?"

He shook his head slowly, but something behind those pale blue eyes of his suggested to Henry that he suspected something.

"What is it?" Henry asked. "What are you thinking?"

Ryan sat backwards, his eyes showing alarm, and seemed to be wondering if Henry had read his mind.

Henry decided to apply some pressure. "Remember what I said to you yesterday, Ryan. If you withhold any information or lie—"

"I'm not lying," he said.

"Okay, well, if you withhold any information from me and DC Nichols, then he'll have to take you over to Bradford police station and start asking you more questions."

Ryan scrunched up his nose like he was smelling dog dirt. "I don't want to go to Bradford."

"Right, well, what are you thinking?" Henry tilted his head to the side like he sometimes did while trying to coerce Tessa into not doing something stupid.

Ryan nodded like he'd understood the warning. "I… I'm not sure. But I think William and Louise had a plan to steal drugs from the party."

"Steal? How much?"

He shrugged. "I don't know. I wasn't even sure they were doing it. I saw her with this big handbag all the time."

"Handbag? What does it look like?"

"It was yellow, boxy, big. I was looking for a cig one party and she opened it in front of me, and I saw some bags in it like…" He nodded towards the one on the table.

Henry thought about it. Louise and William went to the party to steal drugs from the buffet and then went off and sold them. All of it would be profit, and it'd be quite a lot

146

of cash for a young couple like them. He turned to DC Nichols and asked, "What's the street value of this bag?"

He sniffed and looked at the bag like he was a butcher buying beef from a cattle market. "Well, that bag has about a quarter of a kilo in it. If it's cocaine, it'll sell around fifty quid a gram; they'd probably cut it with other stuff first and double their money."

"So, twenty-five grand in total?" Henry asked, feeling completely blown away by the amount.

Nichols nodded. "Give or take a grand, depending on how much they used themselves."

Henry turned back to Ryan. "Is this what you think they were doing?"

He nodded. "I'm not sure, but I saw a few bags in that handbag of hers."

"When did you see the drugs in Louise's bag? Was it at the party last Friday?"

He shook his head. "A few weeks ago."

"How many parties did you go to?"

"I don't know. About five or six; they're every month or so."

Henry considered this. William and Louise could have pocketed a few bags each and sold them off. If that was the case, what were they doing with the money? They'd be sitting on a couple of hundred grand already.

"And," Henry asked, nearly in disbelief, "this Freddie has this stuff hanging around his house? Enough that people can nick some?"

Ryan nodded. "There's loads of the stuff, but I don't think he was happy to hear that people had been stealing from him."

Henry narrowed his eyes and stared at Ryan. "Why? Had Freddie heard what William and Louise were doing?"

Ryan bit his lower lip and nodded; avoiding eye contact, he said, "Yes. I told him."

* * *

Henry leant backwards on the stool and heard it creak under him. He looked up at Nichols who was frowning at Ryan. Then Nichols looked at him, and they made eye contact a moment before Henry raised an eyebrow. Was this detail enough for them to implicate Ryan in William's murder?

Nichols leant over the kitchen island to reclaim the evidence bag that contained the drugs. He put the bag in his overcoat pocket and left his hand in there.

Henry looked back at Ryan, who'd been staring down at the tabletop, lost in his thoughts. "So, when did you tell Freddie that William and Louise had been stealing from him?"

Ryan took a deep breath, filling his skinny chest, then exhaled. There were dark rings around his eyes which made him look haunted by his actions. "I got caught in a room we weren't supposed to go in."

"What room?"

"At Freddie's house. There are some rooms we're not allowed in. It's a whole part of the house, in fact. Anyway, I got bored during the party and went looking for William and Louise."

"You went into this other part of the house?"

He nodded. "There wasn't anywhere else, so I thought they must've gone in there. So, I went in."

"Why were you looking for them?"

"I was bored," he said, though there was an edge to his voice. He started picking his thumbnail with his other hand.

"You weren't just wondering where William was, worried that he was spending too much time with Louise?"

He sneered briefly as he pulled a loose part of his thumbnail off his thumb. "I don't know. Maybe."

"So, you went into the other part of the house?"

Ryan nodded as if remembering what he was saying. "I went into it and looked around. It was just like the rest of the house, really, but quieter and there weren't loads of people everywhere. Then, I heard some talking and found this room, which was like a home gym, with loads of exercise machines in it, and in the corner was a large white fridge."

"A fridge?"

He nodded. "William and Louise were stood in front of it, holding some of those plastic bags with drugs in." He looked at Nichols' pocket.

"How did they react when they saw you?" Henry asked.

"They panicked. Then, when they realised it was me, they told me to fuck off."

"And you didn't?"

He shook his head. "I stayed and asked what they were doing then I saw that this large fridge was filled with tubs of drugs. Like, empty ice-cream tubs. There were loads of them. I don't know where Freddie is getting it… but he's getting a lot of it."

Henry looked up at Nichols and raised an eyebrow. "Looks like this Freddie's got some connections." He turned back to Ryan and asked, "What happened then? How did you come to tell Freddie that Louise and William were stealing from him?"

"Well, we were arguing, I was telling them to get out and leave what they were doing, as it was making me feel proper anxious. Then Freddie walked in. He just strode into the room. He scared the shit out of us."

"How did he scare you? Was he armed?"

Ryan shook his head. "He's just intimidating, and he told us not to be in that part of his house, and then he saw what we were doing. Well, what they were doing."

"How much had Louise and William stolen?"

Ryan shrugged. "I don't know. There were about five or six bags like that one you have. They might've had more."

Five or six bags, Henry thought. That'd be over a hundred grand's worth of drugs. "And what did Freddie say when he saw you?"

"He asked what we were doing, then he saw the bags and I just panicked and said they were nicking from him." Ryan was sitting back on his stool and his eyes were wide and anxious as if he was reliving the moment again. "I didn't know what he was going to do to us. I was really freaking out. Then he told me to get out."

"You didn't stay to defend your two mates?"

His eyes dropped down to the tabletop, and he shook his head. "I just snuck out. I thought, well, I wasn't doing anything wrong, and I just wanted to get out of that room. It was making me feel shitty."

So, was that what had happened to William? He was caught stealing drugs from a drug dealer and faced the consequences. Henry turned to Nichols and said, "Looks like we need to speak to Freddie and this Louise."

"Don't tell them I said anything to you," Ryan said, looking agitated.

"Don't worry," Henry said. "We won't say it was you who told us. But they might guess it was you if you were the only other person in the room."

There was a bang from further down the hallway, which Henry guessed had come from the living room door. There were footsteps, socks on parquet flooring, and Becky Miller walked into the kitchen.

"How's it going?" she asked. She was smiling but her tone suggested she wasn't happy.

Henry got up and felt pain shoot down his lower back and into his buttocks. "We've finished, Mrs Miller."

Ryan leant forwards and said, "Don't tell them it was me who spoke to you!"

Henry glanced at him then ignored him.

Becky Miller sensed something was up and asked, "What's going on? What has he told you?"

"He's been very helpful," Henry said. "He's just concerned some of his friends might not like that fact."

"Well, you won't tell them he spoke to you, will you?" Becky Miller asked. "You'll protect him?"

"We can't promise anything, Mrs Miller. This was just an informal chat, and we are, after all, investigating the murder of one of his friends. If Ryan's reputation takes a knock, then so be it."

Becky Miller stepped forwards, sneering and ready for a fight. "Yes, but—"

Henry held up his hand. "Mrs Miller, what's more important? Finding out how a young lad died or your son's standing with his mates?"

She shook her head as she considered the question, like it was an affront to even ask it, and she was about to answer him when Henry put up his hand.

"Don't bother answering," he said, walking towards the doorway with Nichols following behind. "I think I know what you're going to say."

Chapter Twenty-Seven

Henry and Nichols walked down the passageway. The sky above was grey, and the daylight was fading into twilight. It was nearing evening, and they'd made a fair bit of progress.

They knew that William and Louise were stealing drugs from Freddie and that Freddie had found out from Ryan at the party on Friday night. They now needed to corroborate what Ryan had told them with Louise and Freddie.

"What do you want to do?" Henry asked over the sounds of their footsteps.

Nichols looked at the time on his fancy smartwatch. "Well, I'd better head back to base before I clock off. But it seems like we're making progress on this. I can hang around for another hour to two."

"Alright," Henry said. "Let's try and solve this thing by tonight."

"That's ambitious," said Nichols, not sharing Henry's enthusiasm.

It was ambitious, but something told Henry that they were nearing the end of this. Besides, he wasn't sure he could bear another day of activity. He could feel his hip burning through the numbness caused by the painkillers and his chest was sore. A day or two in bed was in order after all this had been resolved.

They only had two more people to talk to. "So, do you want to speak with Freddie or Louise first?"

Nichols watched where he placed his dress shoes as they walked along the path. "Louise," he said, "let's see if she confirms what Ryan says."

"Aye, and let's see if she tells us what happened after Freddie had her and William alone in that room."

* * *

They went in Nichols' car. Nichols had inspected it again for any scratches on the side that'd been exposed to Main Street's traffic before they set off. He bemoaned the lack of parking in Addingham before they headed off into Ilkley.

They settled on calling in at The Platform Edge to see if Louise was working and find out her home address if not. They parked just outside the bar on one of the town's busy main roads on double-yellow lines, which Nichols said wouldn't be a problem.

Henry got out of the stuffy vehicle, with its minty new-car smell, and took in a lungful of the early evening air.

He was starting to feel fatigue creeping into his mind and body. He'd not had a busy few days like this for a while and his body didn't want him to continue. He needed a nice sit-down and a quiet evening, but he could sense this case was coming to an end; he just needed to close it and be able to back up his assertions with evidence.

They walked into The Platform Edge, which was quite busy for an early Monday evening. There was some dance music playing on the sound system, and the saloon-style booths were full of well-dressed people in their late forties, drinking cocktails and large glasses of wine. Henry wondered why they were drinking so early at the beginning of the week.

He looked towards the black, Victorian-saloon bar and saw Louise and Ben in their denim shirts. Louise was pulling a pint at one of the metallic beer pumps.

Henry turned to Nichols and said, "That's her. Pulling the pint of Peroni."

Nichols spotted her and nodded. "Shall we go have a chat?"

"There's a manager's office down the back. We can ask to speak to her there."

Nichols nodded, and they walked up to the bar.

Ben spotted them first; he was taking a card payment from a middle-aged man in a salmon-pink shirt. Ben frowned as he saw Henry and waited for the middle-aged man to step away from the bar before asking, "What do you want?"

Henry pointed to Nichols. "I'm with a real detective this time. We need to speak to Louise."

Louise placed a full pint on the bar and heard her name being spoken. She glanced up at Henry and Nichols. "What? Why me?"

Nichols raised his voice over the din of the customers' chatter and the music. "Is there somewhere we can talk, Louise?" He flashed his police ID.

Louise looked like she wanted to vault over the bar and run out of the door, but instead she nodded and walked around to the side and lifted up the hinged top.

She was quite short and slim but had thick legs that suggested she kept fit. She walked towards them slowly and self-assuredly as if she wasn't bothered about talking to them.

"Can we talk in your manager's office?" Henry asked as she came nearer.

She nodded, her blue eyes flashing around the bar. "Alright, let's go in there."

Henry sensed, despite her cool movements, she was panicked, so he kept near her, remaining in grabbing distance, just in case she got the idea to make a run for it.

She led them towards the back of the bar where the manager's office was. However, this meant walking past the main entrance, and as they walked near it, Henry noticed her drifting away from him.

He went to grab her, but she darted out of his grasp and legged it towards the main entrance.

Nichols, who must have already sensed she was thinking of running, ran after her and grabbed hold of her wrist.

She spun around and pushed him off her, and he fell backwards, landing on one of the booth's tables, knocking all the drinks off it.

Henry rushed past Nichols and the upset customers in the booth and ran towards the main entrance.

Louise was out into the street in a flash. Henry nearly slipped in spilled beer and rushed after her as fast as his hip would let him.

He burst through the door and saw her running along the pavement towards the train station. He followed after her, feeling the back of his throat and top of his lungs burn.

A few passers-by stopped to watch him run, startled at this old man running down the street after a young woman.

One of them – a tall, proud-shouldered lad in an England rugby shirt – ran up to him, looking worried. "Are you alright, mate?" he asked.

Henry, struggling to get out a word, pointed at Louise and said, "She nicked my wallet."

The young lad's eyes locked onto Louise, and he nodded. "Right." Then he fired off down the pavement after her.

Henry regretted his white lie. What if the rugby lad tackled her? He tried to push himself to run faster but eventually had to give up. Each step burned his left hip even more, and he was on the verge of having an asthma attack.

He spat saliva onto the pavement and became aware of a crowd of passers-by standing around him. "I'm alright," he said to them, feeling dizzy. The pavement danced around him, and he felt like he was about to fall down when one of the lad's friends rushed up to him and held him upright.

"Thanks, lad," Henry said, noticing the young man was wearing a Bradford Bulls rugby top and was just as tall and broad-shouldered as his mate. "The Bulls…" Henry said, almost dribbling on himself. He looked up but couldn't make out the lad's face as the world spun around him like he was drunk.

Then he heard footsteps coming from behind and saw Nichols running up to him. "Where'd she go?" He was wearing his waistcoat and shirt; his overcoat must still be in the bar, Henry thought.

"That way," Henry said, struggling to breathe. "I sent an England rugby lad after her."

Nichols seemed slightly shocked at the state Henry was in and nodded as if the nonsense he was spouting made sense. "Right. England rugby lad." He sped off after them just as Henry felt himself collapsing onto the pavement.

Chapter Twenty-Eight

Henry had been hauled onto a nearby bench and came around while he lay on his back, feeling like an old drunk who'd fallen asleep. He looked up at some people he didn't know, though he recognised the Bradford Bulls rugby top one of them was wearing.

"Are you alright?" the young lad asked, looking down at Henry like he was witnessing an old man's death.

Henry nodded and tried to sit up, but the lad pushed down on him. "We've called an ambulance."

"I'm fine," Henry lied. His left hip was in agony, almost like he'd ruptured something, and his lungs were red raw. He sat up and felt less dizzy. He must have just fainted. He hadn't run like that for years. He couldn't even remember the last time he'd run. He looked up at the young man. "Where's your mate?"

He shrugged. "He went off after that lass."

Henry stood up off the bench and said, "Get him on the phone and come with me."

"Just leave your wallet, mate," said the young lad, looking at Henry like he was a mad person.

Henry wondered why he was talking about wallets then remembered he'd lied to the England rugby lad about

Louise stealing his wallet. "She didn't nick my wallet. She's involved in murder."

"Murder?" The young lad's eyes widened then he got his phone out of his pocket and dialled a number. After a few minutes he asked, "Where are you? Did you get her?"

He listened to his mate on the other end of the line then looked at Henry, his eyes widening. "We're walking down now."

* * *

They'd cornered Louise outside of Greggs bakery. The England rugby lad and Nichols were standing a few feet away from her. There were a few people standing behind them and watching while others carried on walking like they hadn't seen any trouble.

The evening was turning to night and the street lights had come on. Luckily the Greggs was closed, and its dirty, white shutters were down. Louise stood before them, her back pressing up against the shutters every now and then.

Henry walked slowly down the pavement with the Bradford Bulls lad a few paces behind so he could catch him if he fell. "I won't fall over again," Henry snapped at him.

Henry reached Nichols and asked, "Alright?"

Nichols shook his head and pointed at the England rugby lad who held his hand over the right side of his neck. Henry saw some blood dripping between the lad's fingers.

"She scratched him?" Henry asked.

Nichols shook his head while keeping his eyeballs on Louise.

Henry looked at her and saw the glint of a blade in her hand. "She's armed?"

Nichols nodded.

"Have you called for backup?"

Nichols shook his head. "Not yet."

Henry turned to the Bradford Bulls lad and said, "Call the police. Tell them someone's armed outside Greggs in Ilkley, and it's to do with William Knight's murder."

"This is about William Knight?" the rugby lad asked, as if he knew William.

"Just bloody ring, please!" Henry snapped.

The lad nodded and took a few steps back to make the call. Henry turned back to Louise and stepped towards her, while making sure there was enough distance between them. "Louise, I suggest you put the knife down."

She glared at him and lifted up the point of the blade towards his face. He took a step back and looked at the blade. It was small and blunt, probably one she'd taken from the bar, probably used for cutting up pieces of lime.

He glanced at the England rugby lad and asked, "Are you alright?"

He was still wincing and clutching at his neck, but he nodded. Henry heard the other man a few feet away talking to a 999 operator.

"You've stabbed someone in the middle of the street," Henry said to Louise. "You'll have to do some time for that. Even with today's messed-up criminal justice system."

She sneered at him. "Shut up. I'm not talking to some old, fake detective."

"Oh, I'm old, and I suppose I am fake." He nodded towards Nichols. "He, however, is a real detective, and he will arrest you."

She glanced at Nichols and lowered the blade slightly. "Why did you want to talk to me?"

"We heard you and William were in a business arrangement."

"What?"

"You were nicking Freddie's drugs from him and selling them."

She blinked a few times and wiped some of her blonde hair out of her face.

"Do you remember what happened on Friday night at Freddie's party?"

She shook her head.

"Is that a 'no' you don't remember, or a 'no' you're not going to tell us?"

"Both."

"Right, well, we've heard that you and William were in business together, and that you and him got caught by Freddie."

Her eyes widened as she heard this. She glanced at Henry then at Nichols who nodded his head and said, "That's what we've heard. So, we just want to know what happened with Freddie."

She gulped a few tears then wiped her face with her free hand. "I thought he sent you to get me."

"Who's he? Freddie?" Henry asked.

She nodded. "I thought he had people everywhere."

"You mean, you think he's got corrupt police officers working for him?"

She nodded and gulped some more tears. "He said he had loads. He said he'd kill us, and that no one would investigate our deaths properly because he'd got enough people inside the police to cover his back."

Henry shook his head. "He said he could stop a police investigation?"

She nodded.

Henry looked over at Nichols whose expression had changed from being alive in the moment to becoming suspicious.

"What else did Freddie say to you?" Henry asked.

She lowered the knife to her side. "He took what we had on us and then he told me to get out and that he'd find me later." She wiped at her eyes again. "I left William with him. He said he wanted to talk to him some more. I didn't know what he wanted to do. I just got out of there."

"How did you get away from the house?"

"I walked down the hill. It wasn't raining so I just ran down it towards Addingham and got a taxi down there to Ilkley."

"You live in Ilkley?"

She nodded.

"You didn't think about what would happen to William?"

She shook her head and gulped on a few more tears. "I did, but Freddie told us he had police on his pay and that if we spoke to them, no one would believe us."

"Then you heard about William's death?"

She nodded. "From you the following day. I hadn't heard anything from him the day after the party, but that was fairly normal for him. He'd spend a day or two coming down."

Henry looked over at Nichols who didn't seem to buy it.

"Why did you run from us?" Nichols asked.

"Like I said, I thought you were working for Freddie."

"And who did he say was on his pay?"

She shrugged. "He didn't say any names. He just said there were people in CID and higher up who owed him favours, and that they'd not let him get into any trouble, because he knew too much."

"Like what?" Henry asked.

She shrugged. "I don't know."

Henry heard sirens in the distance moving towards them. Louise heard them too and panicked. "I can't let them arrest me." She levelled the knife up towards her own throat.

"Oi!" Nichols said.

"Don't let them!"

She was trying to stick the point of the blade in her neck, but it was too blunt to pierce her skin, instead it just scratched cuts into it.

"You're just hurting yourself," Henry said, feeling sick watching her.

She slammed her back up against the dirty white shutters of Greggs and levelled the point of the blade at her chest. She was about the ram it into her sternum when the England rugby lad came at her from the side and tackled her to the ground.

Nichols then pushed past Henry and jumped on her, pulling the blade out of her fingers.

He called the young man to get off her in case she had more weapons on her, but he seemed too delirious with adrenaline to take any notice, and he remained on her back, pinning her down.

Chapter Twenty-Nine

The sky was a dark purple, and the myriad flashing blue lights reflected off the Yorkshire-stone buildings that lined Ilkley's high street.

Four uniformed officers turned up as did DI Barnes in her black BMW and an ambulance. Apparently, someone had told DI Barnes that the knife stand-off in Ilkley was related to William Knight's murder.

Henry was sat on the back entrance of the ambulance, his feet still on the road, while a paramedic measured his blood pressure. Henry felt the band around his upper arm swell to an uncomfortable level.

The England rugby lad, whose name was Paul, was sat on the stretcher in the back of the ambulance, while a second paramedic looked at the wound on his neck.

The paramedic released the band around Henry's upper arm and said, "Your blood pressure's quite low, that's probably why you fainted. Do you do much sport?"

Henry shook his head. "I watch it."

"Well, I'd suggest you go see your GP about it. They'll probably give you some pills. Anyway, you're not sick enough to get a free ride to A & E."

"What a shame," Henry said, pulling down the sleeve of his fleece. He looked at Paul on the stretcher and asked, "How are you?"

"They said I'll need stitches."

"Well, think yourself lucky she didn't have another knife on her."

He shrugged his bulky shoulders. "She was just a girl."

"Women can cause men the most damage. Don't you forget that."

Henry thanked Paul and the paramedics before he wandered towards Nichols who was stood next to the police car in which Louise was sat.

"Alright?" Nichols asked.

Henry nodded. "I'll be fine. Just old age."

Nichols looked at Louise who was slumped in the back of the police car. "She's coming down. She must've been high on something."

"Think she was using her own stuff?"

Nichols nodded. "She was a bit too emotional. Seemed a bit too paranoid. I mean, to think that a small-time drug dealer like Freddie could have police under his pay."

Henry glanced at Nichols. "Small-time drug dealer? He's got a fridge full of the stuff at his house. Not to mention in his other properties."

Nichols seemed to notice he'd made a mistake and nodded. "Well, you know. He seems small fry. If he was so powerful, we'd know his name."

"Yes. But maybe you're just finding out his name," Henry said, watching Louise in the back of the police car. She looked through the glass, damp with condensation, and stared back at him.

Nichols' cheek twitched involuntarily. "Maybe."

Someone approached them then Henry heard DI Barnes's voice. "Mr Ward?"

Henry rolled his eyes. "I've not got the energy to deal with you."

"Can I ask," she said, walking towards him and ignoring his plea to leave him alone, "why you're involved in the murder investigation of William Knight again?"

"I've been working with one of your detectives."

"My detectives?" She looked at Nichols and frowned. "Who are you?"

Nichols stood straight and produced his police ID. "I'm DC Nichols. I'm over on loan from Leeds."

"Leeds?" DI Barnes didn't ease up on her frown. "I didn't know we had help from Leeds."

Nichols nodded. "Aye, DCI Murphy requested it."

Henry looked at Nichols. "DCI Murphy sent you over to me?"

Nichols met his stare and nodded. "He ordered me to keep an eye on you."

"Whatever for?"

Nichols shook his head. "I don't know. He said you were an old friend of his who might get himself into trouble."

Henry was about to say he wouldn't have got himself into trouble but then remembered he was surrounded by two police cars and an ambulance. "Murphy sent you?"

Nichols nodded again.

DI Barnes was eyeing Nichols up then looked at Henry. "So, you know DCI Murphy?"

Henry nodded. "We worked together for years."

She raised a thin blonde eyebrow. "That explains a lot."

"What does that mean?"

She feigned innocence. "Oh, nothing. I'm sure you two 'worked' very hard."

"Are you making accusations against us?" Henry asked.

She smirked a moment before forcing her pale face to go neutral. "No, I'm not. I don't have any evidence."

"Well, talking of evidence, me and Nichols here have been gathering tons of the stuff in relation to William Knight's murder."

She seemed slightly intrigued and looked at Nichols. "Oh, really? What have you found?"

"William's phone and a bag of drugs that he'd had in his pocket."

She seemed impressed behind her neutral, nonplussed expression. "Where are they?"

Henry turned to Nichols. "Where are they?"

Nichols' face creased and he slapped his forehead. "Shit. They're in my coat at the bar."

Nichols moved past Henry to go get them, but Henry could already sense what he'd find.

"They won't be there," Henry said. "He'll have nicked them."

"Who?"

Henry didn't answer Nichols' question, instead he barged past him and DI Barnes then rushed along the pavement towards The Platform Edge.

* * *

The bar was still quite full, considering that they'd been an armed altercation nearby and that a police detective had been thrown onto one of its tables. Henry walked through the door. The music was still on and there was some chatter, but an anxious energy hung over the place as if the clientele were expecting something else to kick off.

He went to the booth which Nichols had fallen into, but it was empty. The table glistened under the low ceiling lights and there was a yellow 'Caution – Wet Floor' sign in front of it. He couldn't see Nichols' coat anywhere.

Henry scanned the saloon-styled bar and couldn't see Ben. Instead, he saw some other young member of staff in a denim shirt. It was almost like they were interchangeable.

He hobbled over to the back of the bar, towards the manager's office, when Nichols and DI Barnes stepped into the entrance. Nichols rushed to the empty booth, probably looking for his coat, then walked up to Henry.

"Where is it?" he asked.

Henry gestured towards the manager's office. "I suspect it's in the office."

"Who put it there?"

Henry tapped the side of his nose as if the answer was a secret and looked at DI Barnes. "You decided to come in and do some police work for a change?"

She scowled at him. "I could arrest you at any moment for interfering in a police investigation."

Henry was about to retort that Nichols would defend him but realised Nichols was two ranks lower than Barnes. "Well, why don't you?"

Her blue eyes stuck on his. "Because I want to see where this is going."

Henry nodded as if he understood. But what he really understood was that she wanted him to solve the case so she could swoop in and take the credit.

He put the police politics to one side and walked over to the black door that led to the manager's office.

He went down the low-ceilinged corridor. The music died out as soon as the door shut behind DI Barnes, and the three walked along the corridor towards its end.

Henry paused as he heard voices coming out from the manager's office. Its white, mucky door was ajar, and he saw shadows moving around inside. He tried to keep his breath slow so he could listen to the voices.

"It's Will's phone? Are you sure?"

"Yeah, it's his."

"Well, we'll have to put it back in the pocket. He'll know we've taken it if we try and swipe it."

Henry recognised the voice of Gary, the fat, cokehead manager.

"I'll dunk it in water," the other voice said, which Henry guessed was Ben's. "They won't be able to get it working if its insides are flooded."

There was a sigh. "Alright. Do it."

"I'll dump the drugs, too."

"Fine." Then Gary said, "Hang on. Let me nab a bit."

"Sure, I thought you were going to help yourself."

Henry heard crackles of plastic as the evidence bag was opened.

"Don't take that much!" Ben said.

"It's all going to get dumped, anyway. Freddie won't care." There was more rustling of plastic bags then Gary said, "Alright. Chuck the rest."

"What if the detective asks what happened to it?"

"We just say we don't know anything; we didn't find it in his pocket, and that maybe one of the customers took it."

"What about our CCTV?"

"I turned that off when I saw that old guy come in. It's still off now."

"Okay," Ben said.

Henry heard the edge of a credit card scrape against a table then someone sniffing. Gary then asked, "Do you want one?"

"Nah. Help yourself."

There was another long sniff, then Gary said, "Ow. It stings, this stuff. What the hell is it?" Gary started to make noises like he'd just snorted acid.

"Rat poison. Freddie said no loose ends, didn't he?"

"What the fuck!?"

There was a sound of someone heavy falling out of a chair and landing on concrete.

Henry felt the ground of the corridor shake as Gary fell. He could hear the fat man gargling.

Nichols pushed Henry forward, as he was in his way, but Henry held up a hand and said, "One second."

Ben continued, "It was supposed to be William who snorted that stuff you've just had. But I wanted to prove myself to Freddie. So, I went off after him and killed him myself."

The gargling grew louder and more desperate.

Nichols pushed Henry forwards, but Henry held him back. "One more second."

"Just be grateful you're going out this way rather than the way he did."

Henry moved to the side of the corridor, pressing his back against the concrete wall, and said to Nichols, "Alright, get him."

Nichols and DI Barnes rushed past him and stormed into the office, shouting, "Police! Don't move!"

Chapter Thirty

The Platform Edge was closed but the lights were still on inside. The ambulance that'd been further down the high street was now parked outside it with its blue lights flashing.

A few of the clientele stood outside and watched the two paramedics pull Gary out of the entrance to the bar on a stretcher. He had an oxygen mask, but he didn't look like he was going to make it as he was wheeled past Henry.

Ben was dragged out next, handcuffed, and led by Nichols. He was put into the back of a police car, a different one to the one Louise was in. Henry walked over to Nichols as he closed the back door on Ben.

"Did he say anything else?"

Nichols shook his head. "He just said Freddie knew we were coming for him and has gone."

"Gone?"

Nichols nodded. "Abroad. On a fake passport, he said."

Henry tried to think about it. Freddie had already fled the country, which meant he probably knew his drug dealing activities were going to be exposed. So, why was William killed? "Why did Ben do it?" he said.

Nichols sniffed at the early night air and turned around, resting the back of his shirt on the car. He held his overcoat in his arms, folded up. "Ben said Freddie wanted William and Louise to be killed for stealing from him. He wanted to make an example of them. It was Freddie who gave William the bag of drugs, which was actually rat poison."

"Yeah, I got that he'd put rat poison in it."

"William, Louise, and Ryan were supposed to share the bag and wind up dead. But Ben didn't think that'd work, so he took matters into his own hands. He chased William down the hill after the party and stabbed him in the field. He couldn't find William's phone, as it must have fallen out of his pocket during the chase."

Henry frowned. "Ben told me, the night he jumped me outside the back of the pub, that he hadn't been at the party."

Nichols pulled a face. "That can't be the first time that someone's lied to you."

Henry thought about it and nodded. "I suppose you're right. He was having me on." He looked into the back window of the police car and saw Ben with his head bent forward. "What was he going to do about Louise and Ryan?"

Nichols took in a breath and exhaled. "Probably do them in over the next few days."

"But why would he do all that?" Henry asked, feeling at a loss. "Why kill for some drug-dealing scumbag."

"Did you ever get Ben's surname?"

Henry shook his head.

"It's Burton. Ben Burton."

Henry remembered Freddie's real name was Frederic Burton. "Bloody hell. His brother?"

Nichols shook his head. "Son."

Henry looked again at Ben sat in the back of the police car and said, "Like father..." Ben still had his head lowered. "Can I speak to him?"

Nichols shook his head and glanced around the small crowd that had formed around the bar. "DI Barnes doesn't want you anywhere near him. She says if it wasn't for you, we might've been able to save Gary."

Henry scoffed. "He'd already snorted a noseful of rat poison. We weren't going to be able to help him." He glanced around the crowd looking for DI Barnes. "Where is she, anyway?"

Nichols shrugged. "I'm not sure. Still inside probably."

Henry looked down the high street and saw the second police car, where Louise was being held. "What's going to happen to her?"

"Depends on whether the young rugby lad presses charges or not."

Henry caught a glimpse of Louise in the backseat of the car. "If she was so paranoid about Freddie, why was she happy working with his son?"

Nichols inhaled through his nose then exhaled. "I don't know. Good question."

Henry looked back at the bar and the small crowd outside it. "Can I go have a word with her?"

Nichols frowned then scanned the crowd before saying, "Bloody hell. Be quick."

Henry nodded his thanks to Nichols then plodded down the pavement to the police car.

The uniformed officer was sat in the driving seat, under the dome light, seemingly waiting for the instruction to turn the engine on and drive off.

Henry knocked on the passenger's window and the officer lowered it. "DC Nichols says I can have a quick word with her."

The uniformed officer looked tired and bored. "Alright, but you can do it from there. I'm not letting you in the backseat."

"Fine," Henry said, leaning his head through the passenger window. He looked at Louise through a see-through panel of PVC, which was fixed behind the headrests of the two front seats. "Louise," he said, talking loudly.

She looked up from the floor and made eye contact.

"Did you know Ben was Freddie's son?"

Her eyes narrowed and then she nodded. She did know.

"And you didn't think it was odd working with him? You seemed terrified that Freddie would send corrupt police after you."

She shrugged and turned her head to the side to look out of her window.

Henry glanced at the uniformed officer, who didn't seem to be paying him any notice, then back at Louise. "I mean, Ben says he killed William, and that he was planning to kill you and Ryan."

Louise shook her head. "That's not true."

"Well, it's what he says. I heard him say he killed William."

She shook her head again, this time with desperation. "No, he was working with us. How did you think we knew where to look in Freddie's house?"

Henry leant his elbow against the lower part of the glass. "You mean, Ben told you where to find the drugs?"

She shook her head like Henry was stupid. "He showed us where to find the drugs. He was helping us sell them. It was one of Freddie's mates who killed William."

Henry frowned and shook his head. "No, trust me, Louise, Ben killed William. I just heard him say it."

She shook her head again as if the idea was too insane to consider, but Henry could see behind her glistening eyes that the truth was starting to worm its way into her consciousness.

"Here, mate," the uniformed officer said. "Looks like your time's up." He nodded towards the bar, where Henry saw DI Barnes and DC Nichols pointing at him.

* * *

Henry watched DI Barnes say something unpleasant to Nichols then walk towards him.

"Right," Henry said to Louise, sighing. "Thanks for talking to me." He stood up and stepped away from the police car just as the passenger window rose back up.

DI Barnes strode towards him. "Don't you dare interfere any further into this investigation."

"Sorry," Henry said, raising his hands in the cool night air. "I just wanted to figure something out." He glanced over at DC Nichols who remained near the police car that held Ben.

DI Barnes tilted her head to the side. "Really? What was that?"

Henry frowned as he tried to think on the spot. Both body and mind were too fatigued to let him do it instinctively. He forced himself anyway. "Listen, Ben was helping William and Louise steal from Freddie."

DI Barnes's blue eyes narrowed. "So?" she asked, pretending she hadn't started to think how interesting that was.

"So, Ben helps some friends steal from his dad, to set up a side business, but his friends get caught, and Ben sees to it that they don't tell his dad who was behind it all."

DI Barnes nodded her head. "He shuts them up by killing them himself as he doesn't trust that his dad's rat-poison plot would work." She nodded again, her expression showing some slight approval. "Not bad."

Henry took that compliment then said, "But it all went wrong for him, and he's been caught, his dad's fled the country, and he's facing two murder charges."

"Two?"

"I don't think Gary will survive that noseful of rat poison, do you?"

DI Barnes shook her head and looked down at her black shoes on the paving stones.

Henry noticed Nichols was talking to one of the uniformed police officers who was standing near the crowd.

"Anyway," Henry asked, "I heard you were angry with me for not jumping into that office to stop Gary snorting that poison?"

DI Barnes shook her head. "And miss hearing their conversation? No. It was Nichols who was itching to get in. I had to hold him back from knocking you down and running into the office."

Henry looked over at Nichols who was walking around to the driver's side of the police car that held Ben.

"Really? He was pushing for me to go in, too."

Nichols got into the police car and started the engine.

Henry frowned and pointed to the police car that Nichols had just started. "Should he be driving Ben anywhere?"

DI Barnes spun around just in time to watch the police car turn on its blue lights and speed off down the high street. "No. He bloody shouldn't."

She swore and ran in her black heels towards her BMW, which was parked a few feet away.

Henry rushed after her and shouted, "Louise said there were corrupt cops who work for Freddie!"

DI Barnes nodded and opened the BMW's driver's seat door. Henry opened the passenger seat's door just as she started the engine.

"No fucking way!" she shouted as he rolled into the passenger seat.

"Just bloody drive!"

She flicked a switch on the dashboard, some blue lights flashed on the roof and the siren sounded. Then, she pulled out of the parking spot and sped along the high street, pushing sixty miles per hour.

Chapter Thirty-One

Henry's body lurched forward as DI Barnes slammed the brakes to avoid hitting an oncoming car. She then hit the accelerator, sending Henry back into his seat with a jolt. He'd not been in a police pursuit for a long time, but the way DI Barnes was driving suggested she was in one every week.

She had assistance on loudspeaker and was telling them which street they were driving on. A helicopter would be out there in fifteen minutes, which caused DI Barnes to curse at living 'in the back of beyond'.

They had left Ilkley and were on a country road next to the River Wharfe, heading towards Burley-in-Wharfedale. Trees hung over the sides of the road, their branches covering up the street lights.

Henry could only just see Nichols' police car ahead. Its blue lights and siren were on, probably so drivers would get out of its way.

There was the flash of a speed camera as the police car ahead went past it. Within a few seconds, the speed camera flashed again as DI Barnes's car sped past.

DI Barnes was shouting at the man on the other end of the line, telling him to get a helicopter and more police cars with them as soon as possible.

Henry allowed the forces of physics to push him back into the passenger seat while he thought through what was going on. He thought back to how he'd first got in contact with Nichols. Henry had asked to speak with someone involved in William's murder investigation, hadn't he? Then he'd been put through to Nichols. But hadn't Henry been passed around almost every phone in the West Yorkshire police force first?

He didn't know how Nichols had come to answer his call, but what did Henry think about Nichols' explanation that DCI Murphy had told him to keep an eye on the investigation? Henry didn't have an answer for that.

Henry had said Freddie's name to DCI Murphy when he spoke to him, but he couldn't believe that his old colleague was corrupt enough that he would send a bent officer to keep tabs on him.

The car took a hard left turn, and Henry gripped onto the armrest for dear life.

"Hold on!" DI Barnes said, correcting the car and speeding up. "This would be easier if I didn't have a bloody geriatric in the car."

"No, it wouldn't," Henry said, shouting over the noise of the engine and of the screaming tyres.

What was Nichols' endgame? Sneak off with Ben and kill him to shut him up? Or to have a quiet chat with him before he went inside?

Henry felt himself fly forwards until the seatbelt pressed firmly against his chest and his gut. Then he was slammed back into the seat. "Bloody hell!"

"He's slowing down," DI Barnes said.

"I'm glad," Henry said, feeling the dizziness from earlier make a return.

She pressed on the brakes and swerved the car until it was a few feet away from the police car in front.

The police car was stationary and parked at an angle in the middle of a country lane. Its polished chassis and windows reflected the amber street lights that hid behind nearby foliage.

"Stay here," DI Barnes said, getting out of the car.

Henry unbuckled his seatbelt but did as she said. Nichols had parked the car across the middle of the country lane, with its front almost parked on the narrow pavement. He was now sat in the car with Ben. What was he doing?

"Nichols!" DI Barnes stepped towards the driver's door. "Come out."

There was no answer from inside the car. Its engine just ticked along. Henry opened his car door, which caused DI Barnes to turn back to him. "For God's sake, would you just—"

The driver's door of the police car burst open, and Nichols rushed out, running at DI Barnes. She caught him with a punch before he was on top of her.

They both went down, and Henry couldn't see what was happening, his view obscured by the steering wheel.

He rushed out of the passenger's seat, which was parked near the drystone wall, and caught a glimpse of Nichols on top of Barnes, punching her.

Henry knew he'd be next once Nichols was finished with her and looked around for a weapon. He saw a loose lump of limestone on the nearby drystone wall and grasped it with both hands.

Nichols was in a frenzy. He was shouting with each punch, and a string of saliva ran out of his mouth and onto DI Barnes, who was now covered in bruises and blood.

Henry shuffled up behind him, then, just as he was standing over his head, said, "Oi, heads up."

He rolled the large lump of limestone out of his hands. It fell through the air then caught the back of Nichols' head.

He flopped down on the ground as the limestone cracked on the tarmac.

Henry pushed Nichols off DI Barnes and kneeled next to her. She was blinking with one eye, as her left one was badly bruised.

"The car," she managed to say.

Henry looked back at the police car and saw that its backseats were empty. The back door on the opposite side hung open.

Ben Burton had escaped.

* * *

Henry came to. He was sat on his sofa with his hands on his lap. Tessa was curled up next to him.

Morning sunlight came through the blinds. He heard birdsong and cars moving up and down Main Street. He noticed that on the side table next to his green, velvet chair was the bottle of Scotch from his dresser cabinet. Its lid was on, and Henry reckoned the amount of alcohol hadn't gone down.

He felt exhausted, like he could sleep for the rest of the year. He'd got back after 3 a.m. and must've just walked in and sat on the sofa and fallen asleep.

He heard a knock on the front door and realised it was what had woken him. Then he heard Mrs Whitehead shout through his letter box, "Henry?! Are you alright?"

Henry closed his eyes and hoped she'd go away, but then Tessa stirred next to him and, realising someone was at the door, started barking.

Mrs Whitehead started shouting to the dog, "Tessa! Tessa! Is he there?"

"Bloody hell," Henry said under his breath. He pulled himself up, felt all the muscles in his legs complain and both hips, which was odd. He hobbled to the door and opened it. "What do you want?"

Mrs Whitehead seemed taken aback by the site of him. "Bloody hell, you look a state."

"I feel one," he said. "What is it you want?"

"Well, are you going to tell me what happened in Ilkley last night? I heard it on the radio this morning then saw it on the news. What the bloody hell happened?"

Henry shook his head. "Alright, come in," he said. "You can make me a cup of tea."

* * *

Henry put the bottle of Scotch back in the dresser cabinet while Mrs Whitehead was making tea. She talked non-stop then talked even more after she saw the A3 piece of paper on the kitchen table with all his notes on. He didn't answer any of her questions and sat back on the sofa, wincing whenever he had to move his legs.

Mrs Whitehead came back in with two mugs of tea, handed him one, and sat down in his green velvet chair. "Well, are you going to tell me what happened?"

He went into it as he sipped his tea, which was too milky for his liking. He'd finished the tale when he was halfway through the cup.

"How's that detective?"

"DI Barnes? She's alright, I think. She's in hospital but it was just a bad beating."

"And the other one? The bad one?"

"He's got concussion, and he's in hospital as well. Though, a bit of concussion is the least of his worries."

She shook her head. "Silly idiot. What did he expect to happen?"

"I think he just wanted Ben to get out of police custody. That was his sole interest."

"What about himself? Won't he get arrested?"

Henry nodded. "Yes, he will. But it's strange, when you're a police officer, you don't think rules apply to you, as you're so busy enforcing them on others."

"Well, that'll teach him." She sipped her tea. "So, what are you going to do now?"

Henry shook his head. "Ben will be getting out of the country no doubt to join his father somewhere. The police will keep an eye out for them, but" – he shook his head – "I doubt they'll find him."

"And are you in trouble? You did drop a brick on someone's head."

"No, I said the brick flew into the air as a result of the car colliding into the wall."

Mrs Whitehead pulled a face Henry imagined she'd pulled when her students were trying to take the mick. "It flew into the air after a collision and landed on that detective's head a few minutes later?" She shook her head. "Nonsense."

"Well, DI Barnes backed me up. So, case closed." He finished his tea then placed it on a side table and winced. His leg muscles were in agony again. All of them.

"You need to get some rest," Mrs Whitehead said.

"I will," he said, "I just have to do one last thing."

* * *

Mrs Whitehead insisted she drove his car, and he let her as he didn't think he could press down on the accelerator without getting cramps in his leg.

The day was going to be a nice one, and the housing estate was calm. Mrs Whitehead parked his Skoda Octavia in front of Fiona Knight's blue Audi.

The curtains of the detached house were still drawn, and it looked like no one was home, but Henry sensed Fiona was in.

"What are you going to tell her?" Mrs Whitehead asked as she pulled up the handbrake.

"Whatever she wants to know." He took a breath to ready himself. "Are you coming in to provide moral support?"

Mrs Whitehead nodded. "For you or her?"

"Both," Henry said, struggling to get out of the car.

Fiona Knight opened the front door as Henry and Mrs Whitehead walked down her drive. Henry was taking careful steps as he went along, and Fiona called out to him, "What have you found out, Mr Ward?"

The End

If you enjoyed this book, please let others know by leaving a quick review on Amazon. Also, if you spot anything untoward in the paperback, get in touch. We strive for the best quality and appreciate reader feedback.

editor@thebookfolks.com

www.thebookfolks.com

Also in this series

BUTCHER ON THE MOOR (Book 2)

Ex-DCI Henry Ward is woken in the middle of the night when a distressed woman calls him, demanding he arrest her son. After reluctantly heading over to her house, he makes a gruesome discovery before being attacked. With the police stretched, they reluctantly lean on Ward's local knowledge to track down a man with blood on his hands.

MISSING ON ILKLEY MOOR (Book 3)

Henry Ward is taking a walk on the Yorkshire moors when he comes across a child's woolly hat. He quickly connects it with the apparent abduction of an eight-year-old girl from a local town. But when the child's mother acts like she doesn't care, he realises something is seriously wrong and takes it upon himself to investigate.

DETECTIVE ON THE MOOR (Book 4)

Henry Ward is considering rejoining the police when he is asked to investigate a lockdown party murder. A well-to-do local woman's son has been accused of the crime and she wants to clear the family's name. But when Henry starts private inquiries, he meets a wall of silence and will need to use all of his skills to get to the truth.

COLD CASE ON THE MOOR (Book 5)

An unusual spell of hot weather reveals a dark secret on the Yorkshire moors. A woman's body is found in a dried-up reservoir. When the police work out her identity, it brings the past flooding back for ex-detective Henry Ward. He was in charge of the investigation into her disappearance many years ago. Now he is more determined than ever to find her killer.

FREE with Kindle Unlimited and available in paperback!

MURDER ON THE OLD BOG ROAD
by David Pearson

A woman is found in a ditch, murdered. As the list of suspects grows, an Irish town's dirty secrets are exposed. DI Mick Hays and DS Maureen Lyons are called in to investigate. But getting the locals to even speak to the police will take some doing. Will they find the killer in their midst? The first in a series of evocative Irish murder mysteries.

FREE with Kindle Unlimited and available in paperback!

Sign up to our mailing list to find out about new releases and special offers!

www.thebookfolks.com

Made in the USA
Middletown, DE
24 June 2024

56259130R10116